Committing to the Cowgirl

Fairest Maidens Series
Beholden
Beguiled
Besotted

Lost Princesses Series
Always: Prequel Novella
Evermore
Foremost
Hereafter

Noble Knights Series
The Vow: Prequel Novella
An Uncertain Choice
A Daring Sacrifice
For Love & Honor
A Loyal Heart
A Worthy Rebel

Waters of Time Series
Come Back to Me
Never Leave Me
Stay with Me
Wait for Me

Committing to the Cowgirl

Jody Hedlund

NORTHERN LIGHTS PRESS

Committing to the Cowgirl
Northern Lights Press
© 2023 by Jody Hedlund
Jody Hedlund Print Edition
ISBN: 979-8-9852649-6-8

Jody Hedlund www.jodyhedlund.com

Scripture quotations are taken from the King James Version of the Bible.

This is a work of historical reconstruction; the appearances of certain historical figures are accordingly inevitable. All other characters are products of the author's imagination. Any resemblance to actual events or locales or persons, living or dead, is entirely coincidental.

Cover Design by Roseanna White Designs
Cover images from Shutterstock

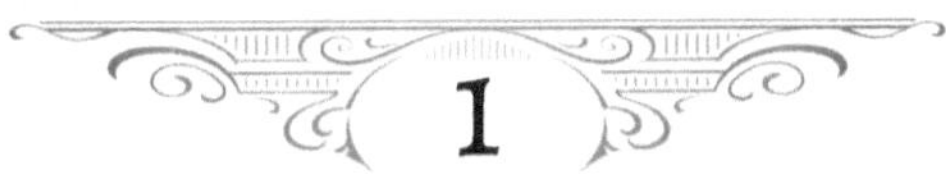

Astrid Nilsson wanted the job so badly she could taste the need for it.

She paused in front of a gray weathered building nestled among the saloons and businesses on Main Street. The words painted in bold white above the door read: *Doctor's Office.* A card in the large multi-paned window said: *Remedies, Tonics, Powders.* Another sign boasted: *Painless Tooth Extractions.*

The rugged one-story structure was smaller and more rustic than Chicago clinics. But the office was certainly better than nothing at all, which had been the case when she'd left Fairplay six years ago to begin her medical training.

She lifted a hand to knock on the rough-plank door to find that it was already open a crack.

Drawing in a breath, she straightened her black hat with its high, flat crown and narrow brim, situating the lilac and plum ribbons so they dangled behind her coiled hair but didn't disturb the light brown strands curled near her ears. She flounced the dust from the skirt of her day dress—a matching lilac and plum velvet-and-silk taffeta with an elaborate bustle at the back.

She'd already attempted to smooth out the wrinkles and grime her garments had collected during the stagecoach ride from Denver. But as she'd walked down the street from the livery, the passing wagons and horses had stirred up the perpetual dust of the high-country town and added a fresh layer to her garments—or so it seemed.

She slipped a hand into her medical bag draped over her arm and pulled out the delicate paper fan that matched her clothing. She flipped it open and flapped air over her flushed face. The high-altitude July sun was hotter than she remembered. Or maybe she'd just become accustomed to the more humid air of the Midwest.

Should she go out to her family's ranch, take a bath, rest, and apply for the position first thing tomorrow?

No. She grasped the door handle. She was doing this now. This afternoon. Before she garnered two hundred questions from her family.

Besides, she'd already resolved that whether or not she was fortunate enough to secure employment as Fairplay's second medical doctor, she didn't intend to impose on her sister Greta or any other family member. Mr. McLaughlin at the livery had informed her of a newly opened women-only boardinghouse at a homestead about a mile southwest of Fairplay. She'd take a room there.

First, she had to convince the current doctor that he needed to hire her, which would be no small feat.

She didn't have to look at the neatly clipped advertisement in her pocket. She had it memorized: *Experienced medical doctor wanted as a partner in an established practice in Fairplay, Colorado.*

Even if it hadn't ended with *No women need apply,* maybe she should have replied to the advertisement and scheduled an interview rather than showing up unannounced.

Tucking her fan back into her bag, she pushed open the door and stepped into the dim interior, the dusty front window allowing in only scant sunlight. The strong, earthy scent of camphor greeted her, as did the lingering bitterness of carbolic acid.

The front room—the size of a small parlor—was devoid of patients but contained several scuffed chairs as well as a bench, and a spittoon in the corner. The walls were painted a soothing light green, and a blue-and-green rug was positioned in the center of the floor.

A half-open door led to another room which she guessed was an examination area, one that allowed for some privacy.

Low voices came from within. Probably the doctor with a patient.

She didn't know the current physician's name. When she'd inquired of her fellow stagecoach passengers, they told her they were new to town, too, and hadn't been able to give her any information.

How many physicians had come and gone from Fairplay over the years? There had been quite a few. But a transitory nature was common in the high country, where people eventually tired of the rugged life away from civilization.

She placed her bag on the closest chair, the brown leather still shiny and the brass buckle polished to perfection. It had been a gift from Mr. and Mrs. Remington after she'd finished her medical degree at the Women's Hospital Medical College of Chicago three years ago. Unfortunately, she hadn't had many opportunities to use the bag, since most of her medical experience after graduation had been inside the Women's Hospital where a bag wasn't needed.

She'd gone on some house calls with Doctor Lawana Lewis, who had issued an invitation to assist in the practice she ran from her home south of Chicago. The apprenticeship hadn't been long or sufficient enough. But like the other female graduates, Astrid had known women physicians weren't trusted or accepted the same way men were and that the battle to find steady work would be difficult.

Expelling a sigh through her tight airways, she paced to the window and peered through the foggy layer of grime at the familiar landmarks—Simpkins General Store, Hotel Windsor, Cabinet Billiard Hall, and more. They were all there, hardly changed since the evening she'd ridden into Fairplay close to fifteen years ago when she'd been a waif of only nine. Greta had brought her to Colorado, hoping the mountain environment would cure her of consumption. And it had worked . . . for many years.

Astrid pressed a hand against her chest and pushed down a niggling tickle at the back of her throat. She hadn't told anyone about her suspicion that the consumption was returning. But she could feel her lungs filling with fluid, and her cough was getting worse.

With every passing week, she'd known she needed to return to Colorado . . . before she was too sick for any of Colorado's natural cures to work their magic again. The question was—would they work for her a second time?

She'd beaten death once. But maybe once was all she'd get. Maybe she was selfish to hope she'd have another fifteen years of life.

Regardless of whether she had fifteen months or fifteen years, she intended to make the most of her time left, and that included working for as long as she possibly could.

And it also included spending her last days close to her family . . .

Astrid stared at the general store, hoping for a glimpse of her sister coming outside, empty crates in hand after delivering her homemade jam and baked goods. The chances of the encounter were slim. It was too late in the day for Greta to be in town. And besides, nowadays Greta sold most of her products to the tourists and visitors who stayed at Healing Springs Inn.

Astrid's sights strayed to the side street past the courthouse where her friend Catherine—Mr. and Mrs. Remington's daughter—lived with her family in a lovely two-story home. Maybe she'd see the young woman milling about town with her children.

What would everyone think once they heard she was back?

She hadn't told anyone she was coming home. Of course, Mr. and Mrs. Remington could have telegrammed Catherine with the news. But that was highly unlikely since Astrid had asked them not to say anything.

Catherine had been a true friend from the moment they'd met. As a midwife, she'd been the one to encourage Astrid to pursue nurse's training. Catherine had made living arrangements with her family in Chicago. And she'd supported Astrid's decision to continue on and earn her medical degree.

Not that Greta and everyone else had opposed her change of career. They'd agreed to it. Eventually. And reluctantly. Mostly because they missed her and wanted her to live closer. Her infrequent visits home once every couple of years simply hadn't been enough, especially for Greta.

Two men's voices from the other room became more distinct, and a moment later the door of the examining room squeaked open, and chatter filled the waiting room behind her.

She shifted away from the window as a tall, slender man attired in an impeccable navy suit coat and trousers led the way to the door, his back facing her. He wasn't wearing a hat, and his neatly trimmed hair was as dark as midnight.

An older man followed him—presumably the doctor. He was much shorter, only a few inches taller than her five feet, two inches. Slightly rotund, with but a smattering of gray hair covering his head, he was attired in baggy, rumpled clothing.

He held a crumpled handkerchief and wiped at clear discharge from his purplish nose. His eyes were red and watery too. He might have catarrh. Or it was possible he was having a reaction to something in the environment. She'd recently read research that investigated the effects of hay and pollen and other airborne particles in causing rashes, itchy eyes, and wheezing.

"Champion will eventually make a fine racing horse," the younger man was saying as he opened the door.

The doctor blew noisily into the handkerchief before

stuffing it back into his pocket. "Good. Then I'll be sure to wager on him."

Despite his condition, the doctor seemed to have a kind voice and personable demeanor. She crossed her fingers that he'd be open to her joining his practice even though she was a woman. After all, a simple town like Fairplay, while it had grown over the years, didn't have much to attract a male physician.

When Mr. and Mrs. Remington had returned to Chicago several weeks ago after visiting Catherine in Fairplay, they'd brought Astrid the advertisement for the medical doctor upon Catherine's insistence. They hadn't known anything about the current doctor either, except their daughter's assurances that he was a forward-thinking man who wouldn't dismiss applicants on the basis of gender.

The doctor reached for a battered felt hat on the coat rack beside the door and situated it over his head. He stuck out his hand to his patient and exchanged a handshake, and then the doctor stepped out the door.

Unless . . .

She fixed her full attention on the younger man as he closed the door, his suit coat stretching snugly across broad shoulders and his dark hair brushing at the collar.

She'd misjudged the situation. Maybe the younger man was the doctor. Surely that was better. Such a doctor might have an open mind to a female physician more so than an older man who was set in his ways.

He began to turn away from the door. "How can I help you—?" As he took her in, he halted abruptly.

Every single function in her body halted as well at the sight of a familiar slender face with a fine nose and a square jaw that was covered in a layer of shadowy stubble. His brows rose above dark brown eyes, and his mouth hung open as though she'd rendered him speechless.

Even though she was equally taken aback, she kept her expression from giving away her surprise.

This was Logan Steele, the son of Fairplay's former mayor. Her first true love.

He'd left Colorado without a goodbye when he'd turned seventeen and she'd been sixteen. Compared to the lanky boy she'd last seen, Logan had changed. His body had filled out considerably. His face had matured. And he bore an air of assurance.

He quickly closed his mouth and let his eyes make a trail down her body before rising and widening with frank appreciation.

Did he recognize her? After the passing of the years, she'd grown up and changed a great deal too. Or maybe he was taken with her fine appearance. She was accustomed to the looks and flattery. Her blond-brown hair, silvery blue eyes, and her womanly figure along with her delicate features drew attention everywhere she went.

She'd been told by plenty of men that she was

beautiful. The trouble was, she'd grown weary of men paying attention to her outward appearance. If only they could see past her exterior to all of her other qualities that made her a good doctor. But most fellows couldn't reconcile why a pretty and fashionable woman like herself wanted to do "men's work."

Would Logan Steele be able to do so?

Even if he did see her as an equal and give her a chance to join the partnership, the real question was whether she wanted to subject herself to working with him . . . especially after the way he'd spurned her.

A part of her wanted to stomp out of the office and never look back. But the other part—the more rational, practical, controlled side—reminded her that this job was her only option. And since she wanted to practice medicine as long as she was physically able to do so, then she couldn't let a broken heart from the past keep her from doing what she loved.

Besides, the past was in the past. Logan Steele didn't mean anything to her anymore. And she'd show him that.

She lifted her shoulders and chin and gave him what she hoped was her most professional look. "I am here to inquire about your advertisement for a partner in your medical practice."

He leaned back against the wall beside the coat rack and crossed one shiny black shoe over the other before folding his arms, revealing gold-studded cuff links. The pose seemed casual, as though he had every intention of interviewing her right then and there. Except that a crooked smile tugged at his lips.

Did he think she was jesting? Some men poked fun at her when they discovered she was a doctor. It was cowardly of them to disparage her education and aspirations. But she'd learned that she'd only harm her efforts if she revealed any exasperation or anger. She had to stay calm. "You do still need another doctor to join your practice, do you not?"

"Astrid Nilsson." His lips lifted into a higher smile, one that had always been a killer. "You were the prettiest and sweetest girl in Fairplay."

Oh, please. If he'd thought she was so pretty and sweet, then why had he left her?

His gaze was back on her face, languidly taking in each detail of her features. "Looks like that's still true."

"Perhaps it is."

His dark eyes were rich and expressive, glimmering with cockiness.

Maybe she should act as though she didn't know him, at least for a few moments. She pretended to study his face. "You look vaguely familiar . . ."

"You don't remember who I am?" Logan continued to lean against the wall.

"You'll have to forgive me—"

"You were one of my first friends here in Fairplay."

His eyes leveled with hers, swallowing her so that she wanted to lose herself there, but at the same time giving her a glimpse inside to his deep, complex, and stirring soul. Those eyes had always had the power to make her breathless and weaken her knees.

Not anymore. She was stronger now. "Sorry. I can't say I remember . . . it's been so long since I've lived here . . ."

He'd always been a dashing and good-looking fellow. But somehow, he'd turned into an almost sinfully handsome man. Too handsome for anyone's good—including his own.

As though hearing the direction of her thoughts, he pushed away from the wall and started across the waiting room toward her, his eyes riveted to hers. Her heart tapped in time with his footsteps, a strange anticipation humming through her blood.

He stopped only inches away from her and towered above her petite frame by at least a foot, just like he always had. Just like the night of the barn dance the last time she'd seen him, when he'd kept cutting in on dances she was having with other fellows.

The glimmer in his eyes then had told her how much he was enjoying making the other men angry. But she hadn't minded—had been too enamored, too easily swept off her feet by the charming Logan Steele. She'd believed he was finally staking a claim on her.

After the last dance near dawn, she hadn't resisted when he'd tugged her outside. She'd been near to heaven with him holding her hand and hadn't paid attention when he'd led her around the corner of the barn, until he'd tugged her close and dropped a kiss on her lips—her first kiss. Even though the kiss had been short and sweet, it had sent her to the moon—no, it had sent her to the stars.

Of course, if she'd been thinking straight, she would have realized much sooner that Logan hadn't been serious. Because after the kiss, he'd spun, walked away, and ridden out of her life.

Several days later, she'd learned that he'd left for the East—without a word, without a goodbye, without a glance back. After their years of friendship and after what she'd assumed was a mutual attraction, she'd been stunned and devastated.

She hadn't seen him since.

During her rare visits home, she'd heard tales of his adventures from Landry Steele and his wife, who liked to talk about their only son who was doing such great things in the East, becoming one of Boston's best physicians. But as far as Astrid was concerned, the moment Logan had left her at the dance, he'd written himself out of her life. And she intended to keep it that way.

"It's Logan Steele, Astrid. How can you forget about me?"

"Oh, w-e-l-l, Logan Steele. Clearly you think more highly of yourself than you ought to."

"I thought we got along rather well as friends. In fact, I'd say we ended up more than that."

Yes, she'd given him her heart, then he'd walked away without any explanation at all.

A long-buried spark of anger flared to life. Before she could rationalize or make sense of what she was doing, she lifted her hand and slapped his cheek.

Astrid's gloved hand hadn't stung his cheek, hadn't hurt, not in the least. But no doubt he deserved the slap. For what, Logan had no recollection. But clearly he'd done something to offend her—a transgression from long ago when they'd both been young and liked each other.

The moment she lowered her hand, her gorgeous light blue eyes widened as though she couldn't quite believe she'd had the audacity to give him what he'd had coming.

Quickly she clasped her hands together and took a rapid step away from him. "I'm sorry. I don't know what came over me."

"I know what came over you." He tried for light and playful in his tone and stance, but his body was as taut as his prize Arabian out of the gate. "You're giving me a long overdue throttle for a wrongdoing."

"Even so, I shouldn't have—it's no way for a lady to

behave." In her rakish hat and stylish gown, Astrid cut a picture of perfection. Although she'd always been stunning and hard for him to resist, she was exquisitely beautiful now. Her skin was flawless, her lashes long, her nose pert, her cheekbones elegant. And her mouth . . .

His sights fell to her lips, the top one with a slight upward turn. Heaven, have mercy. Her mouth was as luscious as it had always been. If not more so.

"Tell me what I did so that I may rectify the situation." He forced himself not to look at her lips and instead focused on her eyes, although he wasn't sure if that was any safer, since the magical light blue was hypnotizing.

She tilted her head and regarded him warily. "Surely you haven't forgotten."

"How long has it been?" He quickly attempted to calculate the passing of the years. But those tumultuous years before he'd left for the East tended to blur together in his mind. "Six years?"

"Eight." The blue of her eyes turned icy.

Why? What had he done? "Clearly you have been keeping track of the time we've been apart. Does that mean you've thought about me all the while?"

"Not once."

"Ouch." He couldn't keep from grinning. He'd always loved her quick wit and her spirited nature.

She briefly closed her eyes, as though willing herself to

remain controlled. Then with an exhale she opened them and forced herself to give him a small smile, one that lacked any warmth. "I have no wish to dredge up the past. Shall we put it behind us and get to the reason for my visit?"

"Ah, yes. You're here to inquire about my advertisement for a partner."

She lifted her dainty shoulders. "I am."

He'd heard Astrid had gotten her medical degree in Chicago. Greta or Catherine or one of the other many McQuaids who lived in the area had probably mentioned it. Although Astrid wasn't related to the McQuaids by blood, she'd grown up among them, had always been close to them since her sister had married into the family.

Blood relations were overrated anyway. He ought to know. His relationship with his father had never been good. Still wasn't. The only reason he'd agreed to come back to Fairplay last October was for his mother, to take care of her during the final months of her battle with cancer.

He was only staying until she passed away, then he was returning to Boston and resuming his practice there with his uncle.

Although he'd placed an ad for a partner in all the local papers around the South Park region, he was actually trying to find someone who could take over the practice in the not-so-distant future.

Not that he couldn't use the help now. As the only doctor in Fairplay and the surrounding area, his services were in high demand. Regrettably, he wasn't able to tend to all the needs, and at times, folks—especially in remote areas—had to go without care.

He dropped his sights to the leather satchel sitting on the chair. Astrid's doctor's satchel. She was probably a good doctor with expert training and likely had plenty of experience. He had nothing against women becoming physicians, had rubbed shoulders with some excellent female doctors in Boston.

But Fairplay was still a rough town full of rough characters. In addition, the visits he made to mining camps and other small settlements were no place for a woman alone, especially a beautiful lady like Astrid. Besides, his patients were mostly men, and they wouldn't want a woman examining them and tending to their personal ailments.

She was watching him carefully. Could she sense his hesitation? Did she realize he needed to tell her no?

He cleared his throat.

But before he could speak, she swiped up her satchel, then stalked toward his office, which doubled as the examining room. "I don't intend to leave today without an offer of the position, Logan. So you may as well sit down and interview me." She disappeared into his office.

He stared at the open doorway, a strange heat jolting

through him. And not the heat having to do with the summer day. It was the same heat she'd always stirred in him—a heat he'd relished but had forgotten about.

Astrid Nilsson had an ability to challenge him in a way few women ever had. He remembered now why he'd been drawn to her all those years ago.

The plop of her bag on his desk was followed by the scrape of a chair. "Hurry now, Logan." She spoke calmly as though he'd already agreed to hire her. "We need to negotiate in a timely manner so that I can reach my new lodgings by the time darkness settles."

Negotiate? He almost smiled, but it rapidly fell away. There was nothing to *negotiate*. He was about to disappoint her. As much as he didn't want to, it was inevitable.

Reluctantly, he crossed to the ten-by-ten-foot room that contained an examination table, his writing desk piled with books and papers, and a bookcase with some of his most important medical references along with jars and bottles of medicines. A human skull rested on the top shelf, a remnant a previous doctor had left behind.

Astrid was perched on the chair in front of his desk, her hands folded on her lap, her feet crossed at her ankles. As she peered up at him past the brim of her hat, her demure expression and the innocence in her eyes only added to the strange heat swirling inside him. What would it be like to walk over to her, pull the pins out of her hat and throw it onto the desk, then drag her into his arms?

He palmed the back of his neck. What in the deuce was he doing, fantasizing about Astrid like this?

This was his mother's fault. She'd been doing nothing lately but nagging him about settling down with a wife. Every day she reminded him that he was getting older and needed a woman.

He'd told her multiple times that if he wanted a wife, he could find one for himself. He'd had plenty of young ladies interested in him during his years living in Boston. In fact, he'd met some very fine women. But every time the relationship had taken a turn toward being serious, he'd broken it off.

Of course, he hadn't realized his pattern until one of his cousins had pointed it out to him. Upon reflection, he'd finally concluded that he avoided serious relationships because he didn't want to end up neglecting his family the way his father had. Maybe he didn't have the same political ambitions as the great Landry Steele, but a doctor's work was demanding, and some days he worked endlessly from dawn until dark.

In addition, he'd been asked to begin lecturing at his alma mater, Massachusetts Medical College of Harvard. Such a post was rare for a man his age and would certainly open up even more opportunities for advancement.

The truth was, right now his life didn't leave room for a wife and family. At least he could admit it. Unlike his father.

The problem was, his mother had grown more insistent over recent weeks, practically begging him to get married so that she could be a part of his wedding.

Just last night, when he'd returned home after a long day, she'd informed him that her sister in Philadelphia had found the perfect woman for him, and they were already making plans for the woman to travel to Fairplay and meet him.

He'd adamantly refused to consider such an arrangement and had insisted his mother and aunt put a swift end to their scheming. His mother had pleaded with him to consider it, but he'd held fast to his opposition.

Their argument had left his mother weak and in tears. And he'd been frustrated ever since.

"So, would you like me to do house calls or the office visits?" Astrid leaned forward and studied the names on the spines of his books. "Or perhaps you'd like to split the workload fifty-fifty?"

"Neither."

"Very well. Then I suppose you'd prefer that I work alongside you until I'm more familiar with your patients?"

He rubbed the back of his neck again. "No—"

"I trained for one year as a nurse, then completed three years of medical school at the top of my class, and have two years of experience in the most modern of techniques and medicines. You won't find a man more qualified—"

"I don't doubt your qualifications."

Her eyes flashed with frustration, but she kept her expression placid, clearly having become the expert at defending her credentials as a woman physician.

It wasn't fair. She deserved the same kind of chance as a man. But the mountain towns weren't the place for a woman doctor. "The population up in the mining towns is still mostly men."

"There are many more families moving into the area with women and children alike. And I just heard there is talk of building railroads in the high country."

Yes, he'd heard the rumors, too, which would make the transportation of goods and people much easier. But the fact was, life in the higher elevations of the mountains wasn't for the faint of heart. "I still think that this area needs a male physician."

"You can tend to the men. And I'll focus mainly on women and children."

He shook his head but was unable to dislodge his frustration. "I don't know how long I'll be here."

"Oh." She sat back farther in the chair as if his confession had deflated her.

"I'm here for my mother. She has cancer. Uterine."

"I'm so sorry, Logan." Astrid met his gaze, the

sympathy within her eyes so genuine he had half an urge to sit down and divulge all the trauma from the past months.

But now was neither the time nor place for him to go into detail about his mother's health issues. "Needless to say, I'm doing everything I can for her, but the prognosis isn't good."

"I'm sure she's glad to have you taking care of her."

"I wouldn't have it any other way." The moment he'd gotten his father's telegram from Denver where she'd been hospitalized, he'd made arrangements to travel to the West. "We thought we got all the cancer during the surgery, but this past spring, it became clear that it had spread."

Astrid nodded, her expression conferring her understanding of just how difficult cancer was to cure. Thankfully, she didn't offer him other solutions or suggestions.

He'd tried every treatment available and more. But it hadn't been enough. And now, he'd resigned himself to making his mother as comfortable and happy as possible in her last days.

But as she'd so plainly pointed out last night during their argument, he wasn't making her happy. He was causing her all sorts of grief with his unwillingness to consider taking a wife. Every time he refused to consider marriage, she had a setback. In fact, this morning she'd been so despondent she hadn't gotten out of bed.

If only he could figure out a way to placate her . . . even if only temporarily . . .

He braced a hip against the examining table. "So you see, I'm not here for long. I'll be returning to Boston, likely by autumn. And I need to hire someone who can carry on the practice once I'm gone."

"And I can do that. If you give me a chance to prove myself, you'll see that I'm capable."

"It's not you I'm worried about. It's the men—"

"I can manage them." She stood, her hands fisted at her side and her expression earnest. She was so strong and yet so delicate. So beautiful and yet so determined.

Just looking at her and the passion she exuded brought a sharp ache to his chest. If only he could give her the position . . . But his gut told him it wouldn't work long-term. "You'd probably have some luck in Denver—"

"I want the job here in Fairplay so that I can be closer to my family." She dropped her attention to the plank floor. Although her explanation was reasonable, something told him she was hiding the real purpose for her return.

"Maybe you can help the midwife—"

"I'm a trained medical doctor." Her gaze snapped back up. "Not a midwife."

He expelled a frustrated breath.

Before he could formulate his final answer, she lowered her voice. "Please, Logan. Please. I'll do anything, anything at all for you, in exchange for this position." Her stunning eyes pleaded with him.

With her looking at him that way, how in the world could any rational and sane man deny her? In fact, he was tempted to get down on one knee and propose marriage to her on the spot, although that wouldn't solve the issue. Except that maybe . . .

His thoughts stumbled to a halt then started up again at double the speed. "You'll do anything at all?"

She took a step back, clearly seeing something in his expression she didn't like. "Y-es." The word came out slowly. "Within reason."

He paused and once again attempted to mentally add together the details for a scheme that would help them both. "No, it won't work. She'll see right through it."

"It will work. I promise." The desperation in Astrid's voice tugged at him. And the earnest set of her chin, the taut but lovely lines of her neck, the slight purse of her lips . . .

Faced with such beauty, how could he resist? "Alright, then—"

"Wait. Who will see right through it?"

"My mother."

Astrid's brow furrowed.

"Before she passes away, she wants to know that I'm settling down."

"And that means what, exactly?"

"She wants me to allow her to bring a woman west for me to meet."

"So she desires to see that her dear son is happily married before she departs from this life?"

"Precisely."

"I'm not marrying you, Logan."

"Heavens, no." He pushed up from the examining table, his voice slightly too adamant.

Her pretty lips stalled around her response.

"I don't want to get married."

She studied his face, as if attempting to see deeper inside him. "Is this opposition to marriage in general? Or merely to me?"

"Of course not just to you. If I were a marrying man, I'd wed you tonight." As soon as the words were out, he wished he could reel them back. Even if she was as captivating now as she'd been when they were younger, he didn't have to act like a lovesick lad.

His gushing, however, seemed to ease her discomfort. At the very least the stiffness dissipated from her shoulders. "So, if we're not marrying, then what?"

He drew in a breath and plunged forward with his idea—terrible or not. "I'll start courting you."

She pressed her lips together as if to keep from spouting an immediate protest.

"Just for a few months. Then we'll end things after

my mother passes on." He hated to think about the day when his mother would no longer be a part of his life. "In exchange for courting me, I'll give you a chance to work at the practice alongside me. But with the understanding that I'll continue to advertise for another doctor to take over when I leave."

"So you'll hire me only temporarily?"

"If the community tolerates you well enough, then I'll request that the new doctor keep you on. But obviously, I cannot guarantee that he'll be willing to do so."

Her eyes narrowed. To hide her ire? And she breathed in through her nose. To calm herself?

He deserved another slap in the face for proposing this arrangement. But he desperately wanted to keep his mother from deteriorating too quickly, needed her to stay calm. And courting Astrid might just satisfy her.

Although Astrid might not be from a prestigious eastern family, her family, the McQuaids, were the wealthiest and biggest ranchers in the high country. They'd worked hard over the years to expand their ranching business, so that now they were well known and respected all throughout the West.

His mother surely wouldn't find fault with the family. And she wouldn't be able to find fault with Astrid either. Besides, she'd always been fond of Astrid, had even encouraged his friendship with her when he'd been younger.

In the tight quarters, Astrid stood but a foot away from him. The glow from the lantern on his desk illuminated her in all her finery and fashion. Everything about her, from her tall felt hat and her flattering gown down to her pointed leather boots, set her apart as a lady of taste and means. She was perfect in every way. His mother would take one look at her and come to the same conclusion.

If Astrid had ever been a cowgirl, she no longer was. Not that he minded cowgirls. But he could admit his mother was a bit of a snob when it came to a potential wife for him.

Of course, Mother might take issue with the fact that Astrid was a doctor. But hopefully she wouldn't mind too much. After all, she'd been an active member of the women's suffragist movement in Colorado—had even continued to use her influence over the past months while she was sick to push for a voter referendum campaign that would give women the right to vote in elections.

Hopefully, Mother would view Astrid's medical degree as something to be celebrated and not disparaged. Either way, his forming a relationship with Astrid would prevent his mother from seeking out other women for him and putting him into awkward situations.

Astrid was watching him with an intensity that matched his. "Let me see if I'm understanding you correctly. You want to form a fake relationship. Deceive your mother into thinking we care about each other. Then break things off once she dies."

Fake relationship? Deceive? When put in those terms, his plan sounded downright evil. It wasn't, though, was it? "It doesn't have to be like that—"

"I refuse to lie." Her chin inched up, giving him a full glimpse of the fire flashing in her eyes.

"We don't have to lie. We'll enjoy spending some time together. That's all. Then when I leave for Boston, we'll have a natural reason to go our separate ways."

"We'd still have the intention of deceiving your mother. And that's a lie." She picked up her satchel and shook her head. "I won't be a part of that."

"You were good at pretending you didn't know me just a few minutes ago." He wasn't entirely sure if she'd been bluffing, but he suspected it.

She ducked her head. To hide her embarrassment over being less than honest?

"Don't tell me you don't want to be a part of this." He held his arms wide, showcasing himself with what he hoped was his most winning grin.

"Believe it or not, there are women who won't fall for you." She didn't spare him a glance and instead started crossing to the door.

He stuffed his hands into his pockets. "Oh, come on, Astrid. It'll be fun. I'll make sure of it."

"No, thank you." She tossed the curt words over her

shoulder as she exited into the waiting room.

As her footsteps tapped a hard rhythm toward the door, every muscle in his body urged him to go after her, stop her—and then what?

He had the sudden mental image of sweeping her off her feet, holding her lush body against his, then bending in and capturing her sassy mouth with a kiss.

No, of course not. He'd never do any of that.

The front door opened and then a moment later banged closed.

He blew out a taut breath. What was wrong with him? Apparently, Astrid's effect upon him hadn't changed one bit. She still had the ability to turn him into a sap.

Maybe it was for the best that she hadn't taken him up on his offer.

How dare Logan Steele suggest she enter into such a ridiculous predicament?

On her way out of the boardinghouse, Astrid paused at the gilded oval mirror next to the front door and placed her Italian straw bonnet over her coif at just the right angle. The elegant hat was trimmed with a wreath of flowers and a net of blue gauze and matched her newest day suit, one that Mrs. Remington had given her before she'd left Chicago. The Basque was a white Swiss muslin and the skirt a pale blue with pleated ruffles.

She knew she ought to wear something simpler, but she needed the boost of confidence the fine garments gave her. Especially since she had to return to the doctor's office and face Logan Steele again.

"I love your hat." The young woman in charge of the boardinghouse paused in wiping down the polished oak table where she'd served breakfast just a short while ago.

"Thank you." Through the reflection of the mirror, Astrid exchanged a smile with the beautiful redhead, Charity Courtney. Slender with almost exotic features, Charity had a smattering of freckles across her sun-browned face.

Astrid remembered Charity's uncle, John Courtney, a gruff miner who'd already been living on the homestead when she'd moved to the South Park area. She'd never talked to him but had seen him around town from time to time. Apparently he'd been one of the first to settle in Fairplay and the first to claim a homestead back in 1862 when President Lincoln had signed the Homestead Act.

Charity had briefly described her history over dinner the previous evening, sharing how when her uncle died last autumn, he'd left his homestead to his nearest of kin—his brother's daughters: Charity, Patience, and Felicity, all three just slightly younger than Astrid.

Having lost both parents to influenza, the three sisters hadn't been able to maintain their home or their father's woodworking business in Pennsylvania. About the same time that the bank was on the verge of foreclosing, they'd gotten word from their uncle's solicitor regarding their inheritance of the homestead. So the young women had packed up the little they had, traveled to Fairplay in the spring, and decided to make a go of it in the West.

Even though they now owned their uncle's homestead, they had no steady income. Charity hadn't said so, but Astrid had easily surmised that they'd been struggling to survive since arriving.

The sisters were raising chickens and selling their eggs in town. They were also taking in mending. But clearly they needed a steadier income.

Turning their residence into a boardinghouse had been a bold plan. The two-story clapboard house wasn't large. But it had three bedrooms upstairs. And now Astrid was their first boarder. She'd taken the room with the closet because she had so many dresses that needed to be hung up and hats requiring shelves.

"I'll be praying that Dr. Steele agrees to hire you today." Charity held Astrid's gaze in the mirror, her big brown eyes filled with both kindness and compassion, as though she understood the difficulty of trying to be an independent woman in a man's world.

"I'm praying so too." Astrid slipped a hatpin into her hair and secured one side of the straw bonnet. "But if he doesn't, I'll be setting up my own office."

Charity resumed wiping the table, its top gleaming in the sunlight streaming past lacy white curtains. Even though John Courtney had been a bachelor, he'd apparently had good taste. Either that or he'd hoped to have a family and that hadn't materialized the way he'd dreamed it would. Whatever the case, the home—the boardinghouse—was well furnished.

From what Astrid had surmised, Charity was the

businesswoman behind the boardinghouse, with a mind for running the place. Patience was quiet and shy and the artistic one who was turning the home into a beautiful haven with all her artistic creations. And Felicity was tasked with all of the cooking and baking and seemed to have a talent for it, if the sweet rolls at breakfast were any indication.

"I heard there's an office for rent above the post office." Charity was fiddling with a vase filled to overflowing with wildflowers—asters, columbine, Indian paintbrush, larkspur, and more.

Unlike the Midwest, where most of the flowers had already blossomed and faded, the wildflowers in the high elevation were just beginning to grow in profusion. The beauty of them was another thing among many Astrid had missed.

"Hopefully Dr. Steele will be more reasonable today." She poked another pin into her hair to secure the hat. She hadn't disclosed much about her interview to the Courtney sisters, only that Dr. Steele was hesitant to hire a female physician.

Charity brushed off a chair and scooted it in. "Whenever I've seen him about South Park, he's always struck me as a kind and fair-minded man."

"I'm sure he's a fine doctor." Astrid situated the pin, studying her reflection critically. Her goal of the morning was to return to Logan's office, convince him that his courting charade was unfair, and ask him to give her a trial period.

If he still wasn't willing, then she was serious about setting up her own practice. She had enough money saved that she could pay rent for a while on an office of her own. She could purchase her own medicines and supplies. That wasn't the trouble. The trouble was that she'd have a difficult time attracting patients, especially with Logan already established as the town's doctor. Who would come to see her? Especially as a young, untried woman.

No, if she hoped to gain any trust within the community, she had to work with an established doctor, at least until people had a chance to witness her in action and see that she was every bit as competent as a man.

Logan had almost given in to her. He'd liked her. Or at least had found her attractive. That had been easy enough to see in his eyes. If she showed up again, this time cleaner and prettier than before, how would he be able to tell her no?

Maybe using her feminine wiles to her advantage wasn't fair. But he hadn't been fair in using her femininity against hiring her in the first place.

Astrid inserted the last pin, then straightened her high lace collar before picking up her leather satchel and turning to face her hostess. "Thank you for your kindness, Charity. You have been a blessing already."

"And you as well." Charity pushed in the final chair

before wiping her hands on her threadbare apron. She opened her mouth to say something more, but then clamped it shut and shook her head as though admonishing herself not to pry.

"What is it?" Astrid preferred direct communication, disliked the games other young women played.

"It's likely none of my business." Charity rubbed her fingernail at a sticky spot on the table. "You're a doctor, after all. But I heard your coughing last night . . ." She lifted guileless eyes to Astrid. "I could give you a tonic my mother used to make—"

"No." Astrid spun to the door, her pulse picking up speed. She didn't want anyone growing suspicious of her condition. Not yet.

"It's a simple remedy, one the Quakers have been using for years—"

"Thank you, Charity." Astrid opened the door and stepped out into the coolness of the early morning. "But I'm fine. Really. It's nothing to worry about."

Before she could give the sweet woman any more time to discuss the matter, she closed the door and crossed the covered porch that ran the length of the front of the house. She paused at the top step and took in the homestead.

John Courtney had certainly known what he was doing when he built the house on a slight rise facing the east. The view overlooked the majestic Front Range that formed one side of the high-country basin. The distant rocky peaks rose above the dark tree line, mostly free of snow. Wispy clouds tinged with silver draped the jagged crags.

From everything Mr. McLaughlin had told her on the drive out to the homestead last evening with all her trunks, John Courtney had gotten himself one of the best hundred and sixty acres of land in South Park. The fellow had eventually purchased more adjacent land in the foothills so that he'd ended up owning quite a bit of acreage. Not only did his homestead have Juniper Creek running through it, but it had a thick woodland that provided endless fuel.

In the early morning, the eastern light cascaded through the few scraggly bristlecones ahead that lined the wagon lane, and the sun's rays swept over the wheatgrass in the prairie beyond, turning the ripening heads golden. The hue glowed with such beauty it made Astrid's heart ache just looking at it.

She dragged in a breath of the crisp, dry air. But as it made its way down her trachea and into her bronchioles, her airways constricted, and a tickle pressed for release. She fought against it, but a slight cough escaped anyway.

The youngest of the sisters, Felicity, waited in the yard among the patches of grass and sagebrush with a horse, saddled and ready to go. A small but sturdy barn sat to the east of the house with a lean-to that held chopped wood stacked in neat rows. A fenced-in chicken yard was attached to one side of the barn with several dozen hens roaming around. Another penned-in area contained a few goats and their kids.

Although the gelding that had belonged to John Courtney was old and slightly lame, it was sufficient for the mile ride to town. And Astrid had offered Charity two bits more a day if she could use the horse . . . at least until she had the chance to purchase her own.

"Here you are, Dr. Nilsson." Felicity held out the lead line. Like Charity, she also had stunning red hair, plaited in a braid that hung to her waist. She was paler and more petite than her sisters, but at eighteen she was already a beautiful woman, even in the plain, serviceable skirt and bodice that did nothing to flatter her.

Astrid hadn't pried into why none of the sisters were yet married. She guessed they'd been too busy trying to survive to have time for courting during the past several months of settling in. They were too pretty to stay single for long in this wild land where women were in high demand. If Astrid were a betting woman—which she was not—she'd give the sisters a year before each was married.

She made her way to Felicity and the horse, and as she tied on her satchel behind the saddle, she could feel Felicity's wide-eyed admiration for her clothing, hat, gloves, and even for her proper mannerisms—which she'd worked hard to perfect over the years. In becoming a lady, she'd cast off everything having to do with the ranch and ranch life. No one looking at her now would ever guess she'd grown up as a cowgirl from a cow ranch near a cow town in the mountains of Colorado.

As Astrid placed her foot into the stirrup and hoisted herself into the saddle, her skirt pulled tight against her legs and thighs, almost indecently so. She tugged at the muslin and attempted to situate herself. But the efforts were in vain. Her stockings and garters were displayed for all the world to see.

So much for wearing her fashionable garments. Later, she would have to unpack her most pragmatic skirts that were more suited to the saddle. For today, she'd have to make do and, upon reaching the outskirts of town, would need to dismount and walk the final distance.

During the short ride into town, she rehearsed everything she intended to say to Logan, still battling her surprise that he was back in Fairplay. He'd always resented his father for bringing him to the West and had made no secret that he missed the East and planned to go back just as soon as he could.

She supposed she'd secretly hoped that once he'd gotten to know her, he might change his mind and have a reason to stay. And after he'd kissed her at that dance, she'd allowed her hope to swell, had believed that he'd get permission to come courting. She'd even dreamed that maybe they'd get married.

Yes, she'd been a silly girl to think she'd have a future with a man like Logan, foolish to believe a kiss had meant so much when it clearly hadn't meant anything to him at all.

The sprawling outskirts of Fairplay near the South Platte River soon came into view. No longer was it a one-street town with the mining tents spread out around it as it had been when she'd arrived on the stage with Greta. Instead, houses of all shapes and sizes lined the various side streets along with businesses and hotels and boardinghouses. The spires of several churches touched the sky, as if reminding them all of heaven above. Not that she needed or wanted that reminder . . .

At shouts ahead from near the livery, her attention snagged on a bull that had broken through the corral and was now stampeding down Main Street. Her heart lurched into her throat as it headed toward a group of miners who appeared to be on their way to work.

The men were talking amongst themselves and weren't paying any attention to the frantic calls behind them or the beast hurtling toward them. When the bull was only a dozen paces away, one of the men glanced behind him. His eyes widened and in the next instant, he was shouting and dragging his friends out of the way.

His shouts were in a foreign language, which meant the men were likely immigrants and hadn't understood the warnings.

Astrid prayed the men would all make it out of the way in time. But the animal was fast and ducked its head as it grazed one miner with its horns before knocking into another with enough power to hurl him into the air. The poor immigrant landed on the dirt street, motionless. Meanwhile, the angry bull charged toward another straggler, hitting from behind and sending him flying against a nearby hitching post.

The bull continued plowing forward, but thankfully, the rest of the pedestrians on Main Street had taken cover in the nearest businesses, many peeking out windows or doorways. Several mounted men, who appeared to be ranch hands, galloped after the bull, their ropes already twirling.

Meanwhile, the huge creature had left a trail of injured behind—injured men who needed a doctor.

Astrid dug her heels into her gelding, urging it into a gallop and heading directly toward the two immigrants who'd been hurt the worst. Upon reaching them, she dismounted, wishing again for her more practical skirt. Somehow she managed to land with both feet on the ground and then fumbled to untie her satchel. All the while, she attempted to assess the injuries.

As the last tie came loose, she yanked her satchel free, and then she shoved forward through the onlookers who had cautiously moved out of hiding. "I'm a doctor. Let me through."

No one opposed her. The sharp elbow jabs she'd perfected probably helped in clearing a path. Within seconds, she was standing over the wounded, their closest companions kneeling beside them and calling out instructions in what sounded like Swedish.

Her parents had emigrated from Sweden to Illinois before she'd been born, and they'd spoken the language around her a little bit. But it had been a long time since she'd heard it or used it for herself.

She quickly assessed the situation. The one who'd been nicked by the horn appeared to have a deep gash in his thigh, but it would be fine with sutures. She was more worried about the other two who'd been tossed by the bull. They could have concussions, broken bones, or worse. Dropping to her knees beside the one who'd been hit in the side and tossed onto the street, she reached for the pulse in his neck.

The man's companion spoke sharply to her.

"I'm a doctor." She kept her hold on the man and found a pulse.

The friend shook his head and spoke something too rapidly in Swedish for her to understand.

"I'm here to help." She hoped the men understood a little English. But from the way his brows furrowed together, she could see she was running out of time before he forced her away.

The blood pooling at the injured miner's side and

into the dirt of the street meant the bull's horns had punctured him. But where and how badly?

She peeled away pieces of his ripped and bloodied shirt and discovered a large gash low in his abdomen. She was already digging into her leather satchel. As her fingers made contact with a cloth, she jerked it out and pressed it against the wound.

The immigrants stared at her, their thin faces filled with distress.

"Lakare." She hoped she'd gotten the word right. "Doctor."

She held the heel of her hand against the pressure point to squeeze the artery against the bone and slow the flow of blood. The spot was slick with blood and bits of fat . . . and his protruding intestines.

"What's she doing?" came the inevitable question from an onlooker.

"Does she think she's a doctor?"

"Women can't be doctors."

The comments began to rise around her as they usually did. But she pushed the pink bowel back in and firmly placed the cloth over the wound to keep the intestines from coming out again. "We need to move him inside so I can suture him."

"The real doc is here," someone shouted from behind her. "Move out of the way."

An instant later, the men parted, and someone

dropped down next to the second man. A glance from her periphery told her what she'd already guessed. Logan had arrived.

He wore only his white shirt, had apparently not taken the time to don his vest or coat in his haste to arrive at the scene of the accident. And he was hatless, his dark hair gleaming in the sunlight as he bent his head over the second fellow. Perhaps he'd still been at home attending to his mother.

He briskly assessed the second man, then called out orders for strips of cloth while at the same time using his fingers to staunch the flow of blood the same way she was.

She glanced around for anything they could use to transport her patient without causing him further injury. Her gaze latched onto a long shutter that had fallen off the saloon window. She nodded at it, then spoke to the immigrant friend who was watching her and awaiting her next instructions. "Board. To carry your friend to the doctor's office."

He followed her gaze and then jumped up and hustled off.

As she pressed her fingers against the man's neck to check his pulse again, Logan's gaze zeroed in on her fingers. They were coated in blood. Then he darted a look at her face—as though to gauge her reaction to the blood? Did he think she might faint at the sight of it? She almost snorted.

"Tell the lady to be on her way, Doc," one of the onlookers called. "This is no place for her."

She was relieved Logan ignored the comments and instead focused on the miner in front of him who appeared to have a gash on his head, probably also a concussion. Maybe even a few broken bones.

Within seconds the immigrant was back with the board. Logan helped them carefully slip the board underneath the injured man she was aiding. As he did so, he called out more instructions for another board and men willing to help with the transportation. Once the injured immigrants were loaded and being carried, Logan hurried along after them, and she trailed on his heels, her mind already at work at what she needed to do next.

As Logan reached the office and pushed inside, someone grabbed her bag and wrenched her backward. She stumbled and would have fallen except Logan was at her side in the next instant.

His bloody fingers closed about her arm in a tight grip, steadying her, and he glared out over the crowd, which had grown larger as people had poured out of residences and businesses to gawk. "Both of the men may very well die today. Their injuries are severe."

All eyes focused upon Logan, whose shirt was now coated in blood. She didn't have to glance at her garments to know the same was true of her.

"But since I can only attend to one of the men at a

time, if you refuse to allow Dr. Nilsson to provide care to the other, he most certainly will die."

The faces peering back at her held no welcome, not even from those folks who'd known her as a child. The mistrust for a woman doctor was clearly worse here than she'd anticipated, even more so than in Chicago. Perhaps she'd made a mistake in coming at all.

"Let's go. We can't waste any more time." Logan spun, and before she or anyone else could protest, he tugged her through the door.

4

Astrid scrubbed her hands with lye soap in the basin of water that sat atop a barrel in the alley behind the doctor's office. The high noon sunshine bathed the back of her neck, and a warm breeze tickled the hair that had come loose from her chignon.

She should have felt weary after the past few hours of tending to the immigrants, but the thrill of saving lives invigorated her and reminded her of why she'd chosen so difficult a path.

She'd sutured lacerations, splinted broken bones, then performed surgery on one of the men with Logan's assistance. Finally, the injured men were moved to the boardinghouse they were living in while in Fairplay. She would have preferred that they stay at the clinic where she could monitor them for a little while longer, but the place simply wasn't big enough.

Logan stepped out of the back door of his office and

approached the basin. "Good work with your diagnosis of the ruptured spleen."

"Yes, the hypotension confirmed it." Along with the discoloration and tenderness of the abdomen.

"You saved his life because of it."

"I'm sure you would have noticed it too."

"Perhaps." Logan dipped his hands in beside hers. They were caked with just as much blood, and as he reached for the bar of soap, his fingers brushed against hers. Accidentally, of course, but it sent a strange charge through her nonetheless.

All the while they'd labored together, she'd been solely focused upon the medical procedures—hadn't thought about anything else, not even the fact that she was working with Logan.

But now . . . she was suddenly acutely aware of his powerful presence . . . of his steady exhalations, of his sleeves rolled up revealing the dark hair on the back of his arms, of his shirt half untucked from his trousers.

He scrubbed the bar against his palm harder, and his arm grazed hers.

This slight touch brought with it a rush of warmth that somehow seeped into her flesh and highlighted the fact that he was an entirely magnetic man.

He didn't seem fazed by the proximity, rubbing the grainy soap between his fingers—his long, deft fingers that had worked so proficiently and with such confidence and strength.

As though sensing her attention, his hands came to a standstill in the murky water beside hers.

What was she doing? She couldn't allow any sort of attraction to Logan to break free of the confines where she'd relegated it.

She jerked her hands from the basin. From the corner of her vision, she could see that he was watching her, his dark brows raised in curiosity.

"You did well this morning." His compliment was simple, but somehow it felt as if he'd rewarded her a national medal of honor.

"For a woman, you mean?" She should have responded with a thank-you, but after the way they'd parted yesterday, she supposed she wanted him to validate her right to practice alongside him the way he would a man.

"I've worked with many men in my—in our—profession. And you handled it just as well, if not more competently than most."

"Of course I did."

He scrubbed quietly for a moment.

She flapped her hands to air dry them, glancing down at her garments and wishing she'd thought to bring a change of clothing. Thankfully, Mr. McLaughlin had popped into the office to let her know he'd taken care of her horse. She had half a mind to have him send a lad out to her boardinghouse to retrieve fresh garments.

"What made you decide to pursue a medical degree?" Logan's voice contained only curiosity and none of the derision that she often heard.

In the growing heat of the day, the rancid stench of garbage wafted toward them from the backside of a nearby saloon. The clatter of wagons and plod of horses echoed in the dry air, and the sound of voices raised in anger carried from the lawyer's office across the alley.

But they were finally alone in the clinic after hours of people coming and going. She had to make the most of this opportunity to talk to him about joining his practice. Maybe if he understood her passion for being a doctor, he'd consider her more seriously . . .

And after the way the townsfolk had reacted to her doctoring, maybe she had to consider his scheme more seriously . . .

Logan lifted his hands from the basin and reached for a towel hanging from a nail in the wood plank beside the door. The towel was streaked with stains of dried blood and appeared as though it needed laundering.

As he wiped his hands, he made no effort to hide his study of her face.

She'd discarded her hat long ago, and wisps of hair stuck to the perspiration coating her face. So much for taking such great care with her appearance before leaving the boardinghouse.

"So tell me, Astrid. Why a doctor?"

"And not a nurse?"

He gave a slight shrug as he hung the towel back on the nail.

"Once I finished my nurse's training, I realized I would never be satisfied with merely cleaning bed pans and changing linens. I wanted to do more to truly help people."

"Why?" He leaned back against the doorframe into the slight shadow out of the sun. Even with his blood-stained shirt, he'd never looked more handsome, his dark hair falling carelessly across his forehead and his mahogany eyes probing.

"Why do I want to help people? Why wouldn't I want to help people?"

"There are plenty of helpful people who don't become doctors."

She met his gaze levelly, unwilling to be intimidated by his direct line of reasoning. "Why did you want to become a doctor?"

"Because my Uncle Lloyd is a great physician, and I admire him more than any other man I know. His great compassion and care for his patients inspired me to devote my life to doing the same."

"That's very noble." She paused, then pushed forward with sharing openly, having no more excuses to avoid answering him. "I was given a second chance at life. How can I do anything less than help others find the same?"

She'd never voiced the goal to anyone else before, and she wasn't sure why she was telling it to Logan now, except that he was persistent and wasn't settling for the standard answers she was used to giving.

"A second chance from your consumption?" Logan rubbed a hand over the dark scruff on his jaw.

He knew all about her past, how her mamma and younger brother had died from consumption and how sick she'd been when she'd first arrived in Colorado.

But what if her reason for becoming a doctor wasn't good enough for him? She had to say something more before he turned her away. "I'll accept your offer."

One of his brows quirked. "What offer?"

"You know what offer."

His lips curled with the beginning of a smile. "Maybe, but enlighten me anyway."

After the outcry and distrust by the townsfolk during the accident, she had no other recourse. Opening her own private practice wasn't an option. At least, not yet. She had to prove she was competent first. Then maybe she'd gain enough clout to strike out on her own. If she made it that long . . .

"I'll accept your offer to have a fake relationship in exchange for the partnership."

"I never said anything about it being fake."

Irritation swelled swiftly, and she couldn't keep from fisting her hands on her hips. "Oh please. You know as well as I do that any courting will be a show for your mother and nothing more."

"It'll be two people enjoying each other's company for a few months."

"And what if I don't anticipate enjoying your company?"

His grin made a full appearance "Have no fear. I'll make sure you like being with me." His voice rumbled, and his lashes dropped to half-mast.

Her stomach fluttered in response—much to her annoyance. And why exactly was she letting Logan bother her? "If it's not fake, then you won't mind if I explain to your mother that our courtship is only temporary?"

He pushed away from the doorframe, his grin slipping away. "She has no need to know that."

"Then you admit we'll be deceiving her?"

His jaw flexed, and he glanced past the roofs of the businesses to the distant mountain range.

What was he thinking? Was he attempting to justify to himself why he couldn't be honest with his mother?

Guilt niggled at Astrid. How could she find fault with Logan for his deception when she was doing the same with her consumption? Sometimes things were better left unspoken. "I won't say anything to her."

His gaze slid back to her.

"I promise."

"Thank you."

"I doubt we'll be around her all that much anyway."

"Probably not."

"So, what kind of time commitment should I expect from this courtship? Doing something once a week?"

"Sounds reasonable. And maybe sitting together at church."

"I'm sure my family will expect me to sit with them." She had to visit them soon. No doubt word would spread today of her presence in Fairplay and the surrounding community if it hadn't already.

He shook his head. "Even though my mother isn't able to attend church anymore, she'll expect us to sit together and will certainly hear of it if we don't."

"Very well. One outing a week and church on Sundays."

"It's a deal."

Astrid let the tension ease from her body. Maybe this wouldn't be so bad after all.

He held out his hand. "Then welcome to the practice, partner."

She hesitated. She didn't want to make contact with him, but avoiding him would be just as silly as holding on to thoughts of that long-ago kiss. More than that, she was being childish. She could keep her touch completely professional, just as she always did with her patients.

She slipped her hand into his and gave him a firm shake to seal their deal. His fingers closed about hers, and before she could extricate herself, he squeezed and lingered, his thumb caressing the back of her hand.

A strange flush spread over her skin, and her stomach did a tiny tumble. How was it possible that the barest of contact with this man had the ability to ruffle her?

Careful to keep her movements nonchalant, she pulled away and reached for the dirty water basin. As she dumped it, he stared at her as boldly as he'd always done, making her insides do another somersault. Maybe she ought to tell him to stop—except then he'd think that he wielded some kind of power over her with just one look, and she certainly didn't want him to believe that. Because it wasn't true. At least, mostly not true.

"We'll need to change into clean clothing before we head out for house calls." He pushed away from the door and entered into his office. "Why don't you return to your boardinghouse, and I'll meet you there in half an hour."

She replaced the basin onto the barrel, again trying to contain her emotions—this time a surge of excitement.

She was finally getting an opportunity to be a real doctor. Someone was giving her a chance, even if that someone happened to be Logan Steele and even if she'd made a terrible deal with him.

5

Astrid was late for dinner with his mother.

From the rocker on the veranda, Logan pulled the watch from his pocket, flipped open the gold engraved case, and checked the time. Only two minutes had passed from the last time he'd checked.

His sights strayed again to the dirt wagon road that led southwest of Fairplay to the Courtney homestead. The coachman had taken his father's newest gig to get her. Maybe he should have called for her with the sturdier four-wheeled landau instead.

Or maybe he should have simply insisted that she come straight back to Fairplay after their last house call, which had been to the family suffering with fever and ague up near Copper Creek.

As with all the people he and Astrid had visited over the afternoon, the family had been leery when he'd introduced her as a doctor and his new partner. They might have more easily accepted her as a nurse, but a woman as a doctor was unfathomable for most.

Regardless, he'd persisted with each family, making sure to involve Astrid in the examination, ask her opinion, and show that he trusted her. And in each case, she'd proven herself knowledgeable and resourceful, just as she had in the emergency with the immigrant men who'd been barreled over by the angry bull.

At the rumble of a carriage finally coming into view, he stood, tucked his watch back into his vest pocket, letting the gold chain dangle out. He straightened his hat and then his tie, trying to ignore a sudden flutter of nerves in his chest.

He had no need to be anxious. This was a simple supper with a pretty woman. He'd shared meals with pretty women plenty of times in his life. And he knew exactly what to do.

Except he'd never shared dinner with Astrid—who was unlike any other woman he'd ever met. And he'd never brought a woman home to meet his mother.

"Is she here, dear?" Through the open window, his mother's weak voice came from the parlor where she was lounging on a chaise sofa.

As the newly acquired Percherons came into view pulling the glossy red carriage, he fought back another flutter. "Yes, Mother. I do believe so."

Astrid hadn't been pleased when he'd informed her

that his mother wanted her to come to supper at their home tonight, especially after they'd just agreed they wouldn't need to spend much time together. In fact, she'd adamantly protested the idea of having a meal with him and his mother this soon.

And it was rather soon. He'd anticipated spending time with Astrid later in the week. But when he'd gone home to extricate himself from his bloody garments after the morning's bull goring accidents, his mother had been so melancholic about his continued refusal to allow for the visit from the match his aunt had made that he'd had no choice but to confess he'd decided to court someone else.

His mother had pried and prodded him until he'd admitted he was intending to court Astrid. Once the words were out, she hadn't been able to contain her happiness. And she'd insisted he invite Astrid to join them that very night and wouldn't take no for an answer.

At the sight of his mother's relief and joy where there was mostly pain, he'd agreed to her plans. And now the delicious scent of the feast wafted out the open windows and teased him—roasted beef, new potatoes, fresh green beans, and buttered rolls.

"Be sure to greet her properly, Logan," his mother called.

"Have no worries, Mother." He tried to keep his tone civil in spite of his irritation at her proclivity to treat him like a little boy. He couldn't forget that he was her only child, the joy of her life, and that his absence over the past years had been difficult for her.

"Help her down from the carriage," she continued, "then kiss her hand."

As the carriage rolled nearer, he moved to the steps of the front veranda. The gig's leather top was down, and Astrid held a gloved hand on her hat—likely to keep it from blowing off. "Mother, please. I do not need step-by-step instructions on how to behave with a woman."

"If you're so proficient with women, then why are you still single?" Her voice rose with consternation. "Clearly my guidance is long overdue, and I'll expect you to follow my instructions explicitly henceforth. Is that understood?"

Heaven, have mercy. He drew in a breath and silently counted to five before answering. "I'll do my best."

"There's a good boy."

Stifling a sigh, he descended the steps and started down the stone pathway that ran through the manicured lawn. His parents still had one of the largest homes in Fairplay, with a spacious, well-kept yard. The gardener they'd employed had planted shrubs and trees to protect the grass from withering in the summer heat. He'd also created numerous flower beds throughout the yard and kept a spacious vegetable garden behind the house.

Logan could grudgingly admit the home had turned

into a fine place, had come a long way over the years, so that it rivaled any of the stately homes in Boston. The advantage of the West was that their property had an enormous barn where his father kept some of the finest horses in the area. Although Logan had taken his Arabian mare east with him and the beautiful creature was still with his uncle, he'd enjoyed getting to know several of his father's newest Thoroughbreds, his racehorses.

As the gig came to a halt before an arched trellis at the end of the walkway, Logan stepped through it and allowed himself to take in Astrid in all her finery, sitting like a fairy princess against the black leather seat. She was attired in an emerald evening gown with all the bustles and layers of a woman accustomed to style and finery. Her hat was the fanciest she'd worn yet, bedecked with ribbons and flowers. And her blond-brown hair was partially down tonight in becoming curls.

She was stunning. As usual. And when her light blue eyes met his, a part of him forgot how to breathe.

Somehow he managed to open the door and hold out his hand. "You look lovely tonight."

"Thank you." She accepted his help, placing her gloved hand within his.

Before she could move, he brought her hand to his lips and kissed it the way his mother had instructed.

She paused and allowed it, clearly familiar with the respectful greeting.

Exactly how many men had kissed her hand like this? Probably quite a number, and the image of her with other men sent sourness through his gut like bad whiskey.

"How is your mother doing tonight?" she asked pleasantly as she stood and let him assist her.

"She's doing well and in good spirits."

As she descended the sidestep to the ground, she leaned into him just slightly, enough that he caught the scent of roses in her hair and on her skin. He was tempted to bend in even farther but instead offered her the crook of his arm.

She was busy fluffing and shaping her skirt, and before she could take hold of him, a cowhand passing by on his horse drew to a halt beside the gig. "Well, if it ain't Astrid Nilsson in the flesh. Heard you'd shown up."

With her back to the fellow, Astrid stiffened, and her eyes widened, filling with what Logan could only describe as panic. In the next instant, however, she forced an enticing smile to her lips and seemed to effectively hide her initial reaction. Then she pivoted slowly so that she was facing the newcomer.

The cowboy was a young, lean fellow with a grizzled face and dusty clothes, but there was no hiding the grin he had waiting for Astrid.

She made a show of studying him. "I'm sorry. Do I know you?"

Was she pretending not to know the fellow? After

clearly recognizing his voice?

Fascinating. Logan started to cross his arms and settle in to watch the drama unfold, but before he could do so, Astrid slipped her hand into the crook of his arm and sidled closer.

The fellow tipped up the brim of his sweat-stained hat. "It's me. Holt."

She stared at him with impossibly wide and beautiful eyes, again clearly pretending ignorance.

"Holt Dixon." The fellow's smile dipped slightly.

Holt Dixon. The name wasn't familiar to Logan. But then again, he hadn't been back long enough to become familiar with all the cowhands at every ranch.

"W-e-l-l." Astrid let her smile rise, but it wasn't genuine. Logan could sense it. "You've changed quite a bit since the last time I saw you. You're all grown up now."

"Yep. Reckon I am. And so are you." Holt whistled low. "You're lookin' mighty fine."

Logan's backbone bristled. The nerve of the guy, complimenting Astrid when she was with him. He couldn't keep from narrowing his eyes at the man.

Astrid's smile didn't waver, but her eyes were as cool as frost on a mountain lake in winter.

Holt shifted in his saddle, his smile falling away completely now. "Lula and me. Things didn't work out."

Astrid's fingers dug into Logan. "I'm sorry to hear it."

"Don't suppose you'd—"

"I'm engaged to Logan Steele."

Logan's whirring thoughts came to a standstill. Engaged? To him? What was she doing?

She patted his arm, as though to direct Holt's attention his way. "You do know Dr. Steele, do you not?"

"Reckon so."

She tilted her face up toward Logan with a pretty smile—the first of its kind she'd given him. At the same time, her eyes pleaded with him to go along with her ruse.

What ruse, exactly, was she concocting? And for what purpose?

Finally, Holt flicked a glance at Logan. It was like the swish of a horse's tail batting away a pesky fly.

Logan's muscles stiffened in protest. Did the fellow really think he could win Astrid without any contest?

If he thought so, then he was in for a surprise.

Logan placed his other hand on top of Astrid's in the crook of his arm and gave her his best smile.

"Never heard nothin' about no engagement." Holt honed in on the intimate touch.

"It's not official." Astrid's fingers still pinched Logan, and her arm brushed against his.

Holt gave her another once-over and finished with a smile. "If it ain't official, then it looks like I've still got some time to win you back."

Win her back? "I don't think so." The words fell out

before Logan could stop them. And they contained a biting edge. What was going on with him? He wasn't jealous, was he? No, he was only helping Astrid with whatever little game she was playing here.

"Didn't know you had feelings for Logan anymore." Again, Holt addressed his question to Astrid as if they were the only two present. "Thought that was over long ago."

"Some old flames are easily rekindled." She tilted her head almost coyly at Holt. "And some are not."

The cowboy's ready response stalled.

Feelings? Logan's thoughts stilled. How strong had her feelings been? Yes, he could admit he'd wanted more from her than just friendship that last year he'd lived in Colorado. But he hadn't courted her because he'd known he was leaving, and he'd tried to keep his ardor in check.

Maybe he hadn't done as well as he'd believed. Maybe he'd led her on and then hurt her in the process.

Apparently Holt had been an important person in her life too. The question was, how important?

"Good evening, Holt." She turned away from the man, tugging Logan around with her. "We can't keep your mother waiting any longer."

"You're right, my love." Logan ducked through the trellis and strolled alongside her. His pulse pounded harder with each step toward the house, and he wasn't sure exactly why. Because he didn't like that Holt hadn't yet ridden away and was still watching Astrid? Because he wanted to know the nature of her previous relationship with the fellow?

Logan stifled a groan of frustration toward himself. Astrid's past love interests didn't matter. All that counted now was giving his mother the small pleasure of watching him court a young woman.

As they reached the steps that led up to the wide front porch, Logan glanced over his shoulder. Sure enough, Holt hadn't budged, and his gaze was riveted to Astrid as if she were a prize mare that he intended to win at any cost.

Before Logan could stop himself, he released his hold of her arm and dropped his hand to the small of her back—a more intimate spot, to be sure. And as he opened the door for her, he kept his hand there, guiding her inside and hoping his message was clear—that Astrid was off-limits to everyone but him.

As he closed the door on Holt, he expelled a short huff only to draw in a sharp breath at the sight of his mother through the parlor door, beaming at them from where she rested upon the chaise sofa. Beside the window. The wide-open window.

What had she heard of the conversation with Holt?

"Congratulations!" Her emaciated face was animated and full of color. And her eyes sparkled with excitement. "You're engaged!"

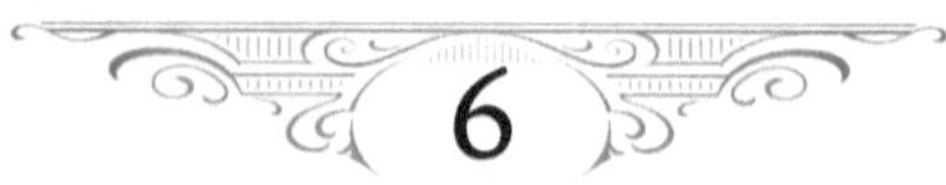

6

Engaged? Astrid almost recoiled at the word.

But the pressure of Logan's fingers on her back kept her firmly in place. In fact, since the moment he'd pressed his hand there, she'd had a difficult time focusing on anything else but those strong, firm fingers.

Attired in all her finery, Mrs. Steele reclined gracefully on a sofa amidst pillows and blankets. She was thinner and paler than she'd been during Astrid's last visit home. Her dark hair plaited into a fashionable twist had more gray, and her face had a few more creases. But overall, Mrs. Steele was as elegant and beautiful as always.

"Logan, why didn't you tell me you were engaged?" Mrs. Steele's smile was so bright it could have lit up a dark room.

Logan's eyes seemed to flash with panic. "Just one moment, Mother. I need to speak with Astrid privately."

Before Astrid knew what he was doing, he was

guiding her through a doorway on the opposite side of the hallway, into what appeared to be a home office—perhaps his father's.

"No, Logan," his mother called. "Please bring Astrid directly to me."

Logan released his hold on her back and took a step away. The dark paneling and unlit room cast shadows over him. Even so, there was no mistaking the rigidness of his shoulders.

"What were you thinking?" His whisper was low but harsh.

She didn't have to ask him to clarify what he was referring to. She knew. And the truth was she hadn't been thinking when she'd blurted to Holt that she was engaged. She'd acted out of self-preservation and the need to keep Holt from knowing how much he'd hurt her when he'd chosen Lula instead.

"I'm sorry," she whispered. She'd been opposed to lying to his mother about their courtship. She shouldn't have lied to Holt.

"Logan," his mother called louder. "This is unacceptable behavior."

He tensed even more.

"I'll confess the truth to your mother—"

"Logan!" Mrs. Steele's voice was turning angry. "You're being impolite!"

"We'll discuss this later," he whispered as he circled

his long fingers around Astrid's and tugged her back into the hallway. Even though he was rightfully annoyed with her, his hold was gentle and as soft as velvet.

He paused briefly at the doorway of the parlor to force a smile before entering and towing her along.

Astrid had been in the Steele's parlor only once as a child, and it seemed as elegant now as it had then. The light blue wallpaper with a white ivy pattern was accented by a decorative white chair rail and elaborate ceiling cornice. The elegant parlor chairs, including an armchair and lady's chair, were all covered in a darker royal blue. The fireplace mantel contained a display of vases and pillar candle holders. And the étagère in the corner was filled with crystal and porcelain mementos.

Mrs. Steele had pushed up, anxiety drawing her face and turning her cheeks sallow. But at the sight of them, she eased back onto her pillows, another smile making an appearance. She held out a hand toward Astrid. "It's so lovely to see you, sweetheart."

Astrid slipped her hand free from Logan's and approached the woman. The mix-up wasn't Mrs. Steele's fault. Astrid took full responsibility for what had happened. She shouldn't have lied to Holt, should have just been honest.

But how could she clear things up without causing the frail woman unnecessary turmoil?

"It's so good to see you too, Mrs. Steele." She took

the offered hand and squeezed it tenderly.

Mrs. Steele swept her gaze over Astrid, likely not missing a single detail of her appearance, which was why Astrid had spent an ungodly amount of time on her grooming. It hadn't been for Logan, although she could admit she'd felt a measure of satisfaction when his eyes had lit with appreciation as he'd helped her from the carriage.

"You look absolutely ravishing." Mrs. Steele's smile radiated with unmistakable happiness. "Don't you agree, Logan?"

"Yes, Mother."

She extended her other hand toward Logan.

He approached, took it, and kissed it gently. When he straightened, Mrs. Steele joined Astrid's hand with Logan's, intertwining the two together. "Go ahead." She nodded at her son. "You need to tell her how beautiful she is often, at least several times a day."

Oh dear. A flush began to work its way through Astrid. This was all her fault for giving Mrs. Steele the wrong impression about their relationship. She had to clear things up. "Mrs. Steele, I'm—"

"Hold on now, my dear. Give Logan a chance to truly express himself. He can be quite charming when he puts his heart into it."

Logan quirked one of his dark brows. Attired in a clean suit and wearing his hat, he did indeed have a charming aura about him. His handsome face with classic lines was the kind that women flocked to, fawned over, and dreamed about. "You're beautiful, Astrid. You take my breath away."

Was he being sincere? As his gaze swept over her, something smoldered in his eyes that told her he meant it.

Warmth spilled through her, and she dropped her gaze. She couldn't let him see how much his compliment and his attention could affect her.

"Oh my." Mrs. Steele sighed as though she was on the brink of bliss. "You're such a lovely couple. And I'm absolutely thrilled you intend to get married."

"Mother." The word rushed from Logan.

"Let me explain," Astrid said at the same time.

"What is there to explain?" his mother asked, her smile firmly in place. "You said it yourself that some flames are easily rekindled, and it's clear the flame between the two of you is alive and doing quite well."

Logan squeezed Astrid's hand. Was that the signal that he wanted her to figure out a way to retract their engagement? Now?

"Mrs. Steele, you've misunderstood." The sooner she clarified the nature of their relationship, that they weren't fake engaged but rather were only fake courting, the better off things would be.

But would they really be better? One lie was just as bad as another. Maybe she ought to confess to both.

Mrs. Steele waved a hand at her in dismissal. "There's no misunderstanding. I heard you say it's unofficial. But that doesn't make it any less exciting. Besides, it's clear Logan adores you and can't take his eyes off you."

He adored her and couldn't take his eyes off her? Really?

She cast him a sideways glance.

He avoided looking at her, but was a flush creeping up his neck underneath his collar?

"Logan, you may as well go ahead and kiss her." Mrs. Steele watched their faces expectantly.

Mrs. Steele had always struck Astrid as a sharp woman. Did the older woman suspect something? Was she pushing them in order to force them to admit to a charade?

"I can tell you want to," she persisted as she settled more comfortably against her pillows. "Go on now."

"Mother." Logan's tone dripped with exasperation. "I don't intend to kiss Astrid in front of you."

He hadn't denied that he wanted to kiss her—only that he didn't plan to at the moment.

Her mind shifted to that night when he'd kissed her outside the barn, how sweet he'd been and how tender. Even if his leaving without a goodbye had hurt, she couldn't deny how special the kiss had been.

Suddenly her clothing and the room and the summer evening felt twenty degrees hotter. She slipped a hand into her pocket, pulled out her fan, and began to flap it against her face.

Mrs. Steele turned her head toward the window. "I'll look away and promise not to peek."

Logan hesitated. Surely he wasn't taking his mother's request seriously and was only considering how he could extricate himself from the situation without exposing the true nature of their relationship.

Because the truth was, she didn't plan to kiss him tonight, tomorrow, or any time over the next couple of months of their courtship. The first chance she had, she'd need to make that very clear and set parameters.

She glanced at his hand still encompassing hers. For example, no holding hands. The warmth of his hand. The strength of his fingers. The pressure of the connection. It was too much.

And no placing his hand on her lower back almost possessively in a way that made her insides flutter. He couldn't do that either. In fact, he needed to know he couldn't touch her anywhere on her body, not even slightly.

She'd be able to carry on the pretense of their relationship much better if she wasn't distracted by his touching.

How had she gotten herself into this predicament? She never should have agreed to Logan's plan in the first place. But she had, and now she'd only made things a hundred times worse.

At a soft rap against the doorframe, a maidservant stepped into the room and bobbed a curtsey. "The supper meal is ready, ma'am."

Astrid exhaled a tight breath. And although Mrs. Steele didn't conceal her annoyance at the interruption, she said nothing more about the kiss as the maidservant and Logan helped her into a wheeled chair and escorted her to the dining room.

As Astrid took her place at the table beside Logan and they began eating, she avoided eye contact with him, vowing she'd find just the right moment during the evening's conversation to slip in the fact that she and Logan weren't engaged.

But as the meal progressed, Mrs. Steele didn't bring up their relationship or the engagement again. By the time the maid brought out porcelain dishes of custard garnished with mint leaves and fresh raspberries, Astrid found that she was actually enjoying the time together. Logan was an expert conversationalist, lively and entertaining, and they fell easily back into the camaraderie they'd once shared.

Although Mrs. Steele ate only bites of her meal, the sparkle in her eyes and the color in her cheeks along with her laughter and attempts to keep up with the conversation told Astrid that Logan had diagnosed the right prescription for his mother. She'd needed him to do this. To give her this gift of being in a relationship, even if only temporarily.

Afterward, Mrs. Steele insisted that they retire to the front veranda and enjoy the stars and coolness of the evening. She'd forced them to go on without her, assuring them that she'd join them later.

With the moonlight illuminating the veranda along with the glow of the windows behind them, Astrid settled into a chair next to Logan, and they shared an easy discussion about their experiences at medical school, comparing the classes they'd taken and the number of dissections they'd experienced along with the hardest cases they'd had.

She found herself telling him about her work on the women's syphilitic ward and the horrible situations she'd encountered there with women devastated by venereal diseases, servants who'd been impregnated by their employers, and even those patients driven to mental illness by their unfortunate circumstances.

He was an astute listener, full of insightful comments and direct questions. He shared his own hardships, particularly his work among some of the poorest immigrants. He clearly loved practicing with his uncle and missed the work and couldn't wait to finally return to Boston. He hoped to be back by autumn because he'd been asked to give lectures at Mass Medical College, which was a prestigious opportunity for him.

They talked for hours, until finally the coldness of the night made her shiver. He quickly stood and gave her his coat. Only then did they realize his mother hadn't come out. Upon inquiring after her with one of the servants, they learned she'd gone to bed right after their meal.

Since the hour was late, Logan drove her home. As the boardinghouse came into view, she cringed at the sight of the windows all dark except for a light glowing in her upstairs bedroom window.

"I feel bad that I lost track of the time." In the morning, she would have to apologize to Charity for not returning at an earlier hour.

"Is that your way of saying you had a good time this evening?" He slowed the gig so that the quiet of the night settled about them, the soft jangle of the harness mingling with the trill of crickets.

She twisted on the seat to face him, still wearing his coat after he'd donned another. The broadness of it swallowed her up, but she didn't mind. A part of her could even admit she liked the earthy spiciness of his cologne that lingered in the fabric.

He lifted off his simple black derby as he guided the gig down the dirt lane toward the now-silent two-story home, and the night breeze tousled his hair. Both his shoulders and face contained peacefulness, as though he'd forgotten for just a short while about his mother's illness and all his responsibilities.

"I did have a good time," she said softly.

He cast her a sideways glance. "I have no trouble admitting to the same."

"I'm likely the most interesting woman you've ever courted."

"Yes." He chuckled. "I've never discussed foot dissections with any other woman."

She smiled. "Or how to treat obstinate constipation."

"Very true."

As he reached the house and brought the gig to a halt, she started to shed the coat.

"Astrid, wait." His voice held a note of pleading.

Even though she'd enjoyed talking with him all evening, she'd known she couldn't avoid the coming conversation forever, the one in which they discussed what had happened with Holt.

She might as well get right to it. "I'm sorry for lying to Holt about being engaged to you."

He fingered the brim of his hat, silent for a moment, as though not quite sure what to do with her frank apology. "I'm curious why you wanted him to think we're engaged." His tone was absent the frustration that had been there earlier. Perhaps he'd realized a fake engagement hadn't amounted to much trouble after all since his mother had only emphasized it initially and then hadn't brought it up again. "Tell me about him."

"Holt and I courted before I left for Chicago."

"I gathered that."

The thought of all that had happened with Holt didn't hurt the same way it used to. And even though she'd been startled to see him tonight, the sight hadn't elicited the same pain that it had the other visits home.

"We corresponded the first year while I was doing nursing training. We'd made plans to get married once I finished and came home—"

"Then you were engaged to him?" Logan's voice rose with surprise.

"Not formally. But I thought we had an understanding. I was nearing the end of my training when I received a letter from one of my friends letting me know Holt was courting someone else."

"He didn't have the backbone to tell you himself?"

"He was completely spineless." She peered up at the cloudless sky overhead and the clarity and vastness of the stars—something else she'd missed about the West. "He actually did me a favor. After the letter, I decided to stay in Chicago, and that's when I realized I'd rather get my medical degree."

"Perhaps tonight you should have thanked him instead of announcing our engagement."

A bitter laugh escaped. "When I came home for a visit after completing my first year of medical school, he stopped me. On the street. In public. And told me he was engaged."

"Ah." The one word expressed both understanding and compassion. "From the way he talked tonight, it appears he regrets giving you up."

"I was hoping he'd feel that way. And I guess I couldn't resist giving him a taste of his own medicine."

"You did do that."

"I didn't want him to think I was still unattached and pining away after him. I wanted him to think I've moved on."

"And have you moved on?" He slid a sideways glance her way.

"Is this the part of the conversation where you're trying to figure out if I'm free of romantic entanglements with anyone else?" She didn't give him the chance to respond. "It's a little late for that, isn't it? Now that we're courting?"

"And engaged." This time his tone was filled with mirth.

There were many things she'd always liked about Logan Steele. His ability to find humor in difficult situations was one of her favorites. Even if he could make light of what had happened, she had to figure out a way to undo the engagement. "Again, I'm sorry for lying. I'll make a point of riding out to the ranch where Holt works and setting him straight."

"No. Don't do that."

"I insist."

"And so do I." He started to reach across the seat as though he meant to take her hand, but then he latched onto his hat again. "That fellow was a complete blockhead and doesn't deserve a woman like you. Let him feel the pain of his loss."

"He'll find out soon anyway. Once you leave. Everyone will think I've been rejected by another man, and Holt will just feel sorry for me."

"That will be a problem." Logan's brow furrowed, and he peered unseeingly at the dark outline of the foothills beyond the house. "How about after my mother passes, you stage a breakup and reject me? Then no one has to feel sorry for you."

She let his idea bounce around in her mind. "It might work."

"Except that Dolt—"

"Holt."

"Dolt." His lips curved up into a grin.

She bit back one of her own.

"Dolt will come calling on you the minute I board the stagecoach. In fact, I think the fellow is planning to come calling even though we're engaged."

"Fake engaged."

"He won't have to know it."

"So you don't want me to clear up the fake engagement with him?"

He hesitated. "I guess it's not much different than a

fake courtship."

"True. And I did make it clear that the engagement isn't official."

"What exactly is an official engagement?"

"It means we've talked about marriage, but you haven't actually gotten down on one knee and proposed." She'd expected him to have a wife by now, as handsome and charming as he was. But from the way he'd spoken yesterday about not having any intention of getting married, she guessed he'd either been hurt or lost someone he loved and was now ruined for any other woman.

"Official or not, he'd better not set his sights on having you. Not while I'm around."

This time she couldn't keep her smile back. "Do I detect jealousy?"

"Fake jealousy."

She laughed.

His grin widened. "You're my fake almost-fiancée, so I have every right to feel fake almost-jealousy."

A strange giddiness floated through her. When she slapped him yesterday in his office, she never would have imagined that one day later she'd be sitting in the dark enjoying his company this much.

She had to be careful. He was too easy to like. She'd learned that long ago. He was also too ready to leave. Another thing she'd learned long ago.

She scooted toward the door of the gig. "I won't say anything to Holt. But I will apologize to your mother and explain myself to her."

He reached out and touched her arm.

The soft brush sent her heartbeat into a stuttering patter, and her gaze darted down to where his fingers lay.

He dropped his hand and rested it on the seat beside her, which was still too near. "We don't need to say anything more to her for now."

"I already feel bad enough for deceiving her as it is. I can't add to that."

He was silent a moment, then nodded. "Then I'll talk to her tomorrow and set her straight."

She stood to climb down, but before she could maneuver the layers of her skirts and find the step, he'd already hopped out and bounded around to her side. She accepted his hand, knowing he was only being polite. Even so, she was much too aware of the smooth, taut texture of his skin and suddenly needed to put as much distance between them as possible.

Once her feet were firmly on the ground, she pulled away and started at a brisk pace to the house. "Thank you for a lovely evening." She tossed the parting comment over her shoulder.

He didn't move, his gaze riveted to her, undisguised interest in his eyes.

With her heart picking up its pace, she hurried up the

steps and across the porch. When she was finally inside the dark front room with the door closed behind her, she leaned back against it and pressed a hand against the wild thudding in her chest.

Why was she allowing Logan to rattle her? She was no longer a naïve and inexperienced girl on the cusp of womanhood. No, she was mature and knowledgeable enough to understand that she'd only suffer another heartbreak if she allowed herself to care for Logan again.

She couldn't. He had to remain her partner in work and nothing more. That was all there was to it.

7

Logan could admit Astrid was an exceptionally fine doctor. All morning he'd stood aside and let her diagnose each patient who came into the office. And each time, she'd been correct about the ailment and the corresponding treatment.

During the afternoon, they'd made house calls, mostly around Fairplay. Again, he'd involved her as much as possible, seeking her opinion and advice—although he'd needed neither. But in doing so, he'd tried to show folks that he respected and valued her as a doctor. And he hoped eventually, they would learn to do so as well.

"Give it more time." Side by side, they walked away from the dilapidated tenement homes where the immigrants lived. Among others, they'd visited the two men injured by the bull. Both were conscious and in a great deal of pain. He and Astrid had cleaned and dressed their wounds, then given them more opium to ease their discomfort.

"It's a continual battle to be accepted." Her stride was long and purposeful, her boots echoing a hard thud against the plank sidewalk that ran the length of Main Street.

He hardly had to slow his steps to match hers. In fact, he had half a mind to go faster just so they could avoid the attention she was drawing. The traffic had grown heavier with the coming of the evening and the men swelling into town to dine at the restaurants and visit the saloons. And those men were much too interested in Astrid.

He couldn't fault them for their fascination. Even though she was attired in a practical blue skirt and matching bodice and simple hat, she was as pretty today as she'd been last night in all her finery. Apparently, every man in town thought so, too, and wanted a look at Fairplay's new striking beauty.

As they passed by the open door of one of the saloons, suggestive whistles came from inside, along with, "If the little lady doctor needs someone to examine, I'll volunteer."

His steps fumbled to a halt, and his fingers went to the revolver holstered underneath his coat.

"Don't let it bother you." Astrid placed a hand on his arm. "I'm used to those kinds of comments from ruffians who have no regard for women with professions."

"The men in this town need to know they can't talk

that way about you."

"Nothing you say or do will make a difference." She tugged him forward, giving him little choice but to move past the saloon. "Only I can prove myself, and as you pointed out, that will take some time."

The raucous laughter from within the saloon—likely another bawdy comment—trailed them. Men stood outside the barber shop and gawked as Astrid passed. Others poked their heads out windows. The fellows playing checkers outside of Simpkins also paused in their game to watch her.

She passed by them without a glance, swinging her doctor's bag at her side. If he hadn't watched her at work again today, he wouldn't have believed a woman as young as Astrid could be such a talented doctor.

But she was very talented. And he was resolved more than ever, especially after her cooperation to make his mother happy, to help her gain her footing in the community so that whoever took over the practice would look favorably upon her and accept her as a partner.

Unfortunately, he suspected that even if she proved she was the best doctor in all of Colorado, most male physicians would still balk at the prospect of having her in their practice. Obviously, he'd hesitated initially, and he considered himself one of the more open-minded of his sex.

"Astrid Nilsson!" A woman standing beside a wagon

parked in front of the medical clinic waved at them.

Astrid's steps slowed for just a moment before she started forward again faster, a smile lighting up her face. As she dodged past others on the walkway, Logan followed on her heels. And as they finally reached the wagon, she launched herself in the most unladylike of manners against a slender woman of the same fair hair and silvery blue eye coloring.

Greta McQuaid. Astrid's sister. Logan had actually just seen one of her energetic little boys last week to remove a fishing hook from his arm. He wasn't sure how many children Greta and her husband Wyatt had, but it was at least half a dozen. Several of them were peeking over the edge of the wagon bed.

"Greta!" The sisters hugged each other tightly. Older than Astrid by at least a decade, Greta was still a fine-looking woman and an even finer businesswoman.

After exchanging greetings with her sister, Astrid turned to hug the children. Then she hugged Greta again.

"Ty told me you were here." Greta pulled back and held Astrid at arm's length, studying her with eyes that were almost as pretty as Astrid's but not quite. "He drove into town earlier this afternoon to drop off some of my products. And he heard news that there was a new doctor in town. You."

Logan had seen Tyler McQuaid, Greta's oldest son, around town from time to time, a stocky and fine-looking lad who was fast growing into a man.

"Yes, it's me." Astrid's smile was so genuine and full of love that Logan wanted to have a portrait painted of her right here and now to capture that expression.

"You should have told me you were coming home." Greta pulled Astrid back into a hug and squeezed her hard. As she did so, her gaze snagged upon him standing but a few feet away, and her brows quirked with curiosity.

Of course she'd have to catch him in the act of admiring Astrid. Logan shifted toward the door. From what he could see through the dusty window into the waiting room, he didn't have any patients awaiting his return. He'd close up and head home.

"We're done for the day, Astrid." He reached for the door. "Go on and spend some time with your family."

"From the news Ty brought home"—Greta released Astrid and took a step after him—"it sounds like you're going to be family soon, Dr. Steele."

Hand on the doorknob, Logan stilled. Family? Soon? Her declaration could only mean one thing. Word about their fake engagement had spread. And since only two people besides themselves knew about their fake engagement, he could easily narrow down who'd spread the word. His mother.

She'd been asleep when he'd returned last night after dropping Astrid off at her boardinghouse. And she'd still been asleep when he'd left for the office this morning. So he hadn't had the opportunity to set her straight about the *miscommunication*. He'd intended to speak to her more about it tonight and let her know the partial truth—that Astrid had brought up the engagement because of Holt and not because they were really engaged.

But now . . . he was too late.

The clatter of a passing wagon, the bang of a door, the shouts of greetings, the laughter of children playing nearby—all the familiar noises of the town around him rivaled the clamor in his head, which was growing louder by the second.

What could he do to stop the rumor of his and Astrid's engagement from spreading even farther? He had to put an end to it. Before it got out of hand, if it hadn't already.

Stiffening his vertebrae with resolve, he spun to find Astrid's wide eyes upon him and urging him to use caution.

"When did you get engaged?" Greta's gaze bounced back and forth between them before landing on Astrid. "I didn't even know you'd kept in touch with Logan—Dr. Steele."

"We haven't really corresponded," Astrid started. "And we're actually not officially engaged."

"But Mrs. Steele has issued invitations to the entire town and surrounding community to an engagement party at her home this coming Saturday evening."

Logan's blood turned to ice, and his heart crashed to a halt, like a ship hitting an iceberg. What had his mother done?

"A party?" Astrid's tone rose a notch. "Mrs. Steele didn't mention anything about a party last night at supper."

"Yes, I heard you shared a meal with the Steeles last night." Greta's statement didn't contain accusation, only curiosity.

No doubt Greta was wondering why Astrid had made time for his family but hadn't visited her own sister yet.

"Is everything about my life public knowledge?" Astrid slanted Logan a look, as if he were at fault. Which he was. He'd been the one to start the whole relationship pretense.

He opened his mouth to apologize, but Greta spoke first. "I also learned you're staying at the Courtneys' new boardinghouse instead of living with us."

"I can explain."

Greta fished in her skirt pocket and pulled out a half sheet with bold print splashed across it, then pushed the half sheet in front of Astrid. "I just wish you would have told me about you and Logan personally so that I didn't have to hear it first from this."

Astrid took the paper, and as she read it, her eyes froze into a wintery silver. "Logan?" Her voice quavered. "May I speak with you privately?"

He wanted to tell her no. But why delay the inevitable? "Of course." He finished opening the door and then waved her inside.

She narrowed her eyes at him as if to tell him the discussion wouldn't be pleasant. Then she offered her sister a half smile. "I'm sorry, Greta. I'll tell you everything later."

"Supper will be ready soon." Greta smiled warmly in return, clearly not willing to hold on to any grudges. "You and Logan must come."

"I'll come alone."

"No, we want Logan to as well. Since he's to be a part of your life, we'd like the chance to get to know him better."

From the tension radiating from Astrid, he knew she didn't want him to be a part of her family meal. And he didn't blame her. She wanted to keep this business arrangement with him separate from her private and family life. "Thank you for the kind invitation, Mrs. McQuaid. But Astrid needs some time alone with her family tonight. I'll visit another evening, if you'll have me."

"Nonsense." Greta waved a dismissive hand. "Astrid had supper with your mother last night. It's only fair that we get the two of you tonight. Catherine and Dylan will be over shortly to get you."

Without giving them a chance to protest any further,

Greta pressed a kiss to Astrid's forehead before climbing up onto the wagon bench. The curious faces of her youngest children peered over the edge of the back at them.

Astrid didn't wait for her sister to drive away before storming toward him. As she stepped past him, she latched onto his arm and drew him inside. After closing the door, she dragged him toward the examining room.

He let her lead him, his whole body thrumming with anticipation at what this feisty woman intended to do to him.

She halted before entering, dropped her satchel, and spun to face him, releasing him in the process and fisting her hands at her sides. "Logan Steele." She was the most beautiful creature he'd ever laid eyes on with her cheeks flushed, her eyes sparkling, and her body taut.

He had a sudden overpowering need to grab her and yank her flush against him. His muscles tightened just thinking about holding her like that.

"You're in big trouble." She lowered her voice and cast a glance toward the front window as though perhaps Greta might be lurking outside, attempting to overhear their conversation.

He set down his satchel, too, then leaned his shoulder against the doorframe opposite her and tried to ease the strong need for her out of his body. He couldn't let his thoughts start down a road that would dead-end.

He'd be better off apologizing profusely to her that he'd neglected to correct his mother's misunderstanding about them. Then he'd offer to climb out onto the second-floor balcony of the nearest hotel and make a public announcement that he wasn't engaged to her.

But as she pursed her lips with displeasure, her adorable upper lip seemed to beg him for a kiss, which only fanned heat inside him. "What kind of trouble am I in?"

"Clearly you didn't talk to your mother last night like you said you would."

"She was asleep when I got home. It was rather late, you know." He couldn't keep the teasing from his tone.

"This isn't a joking matter, Logan." Her voice rose a notch, but then she lowered it to a harsh whisper. "You have to stop her from throwing that party."

"I can't stop my mother from doing anything. She has a mind of her own."

"You have to try." She stepped closer, only an arm's length away. "This has gotten out of hand."

He crossed his arms to keep himself from reaching for her.

"If you don't tell her to cancel it, then I will."

"Alright. We can go together and tell her we're not engaged, but only if you promise not to say anything about our courtship."

"Fine. But once we do that, I'm going out to my

family's dinner by myself."

"What will Greta say when you show up without me?"

"I'll explain everything to her too." She spun with enough spitfire in her step to incinerate anyone near her.

At the very least, she had the power to incinerate his rational thinking. Before she could make it two paces away, he latched on to her upper arm and dragged her back toward him. "Wait."

She stumbled, then toppled into him.

Her curvy body pressed against him just the way he'd imagined. And instead of pushing back and straightening, she grew motionless except for her fingers fisting in his coat. She tugged harder, as if she wanted to gather more of him.

Heaven, have mercy. Astrid Nilsson was a fine, fine woman.

She stared straight ahead at his shirt, shifting up to his necktie. Then she darted a glance at his mouth.

Another jolt of desire shot through him.

What was she thinking? Of kissing him? Was she attracted to him more than she'd let on?

Before he could talk himself out of anything, he lifted a hand to her cheek and brushed back a strand of her hair.

At the graze of his finger, she drew in a shaky breath, and her lashes fell halfway.

Ah, yes. She most definitely was experiencing

something for him. Whatever it was, he couldn't deny that he liked her.

Was this how it had been between them before he left? The attraction? The magnetic tension? The need?

If so, maybe it was a good thing he'd left when he had. Who knew what kind of trouble or heartache he would have caused her, especially because he'd been so young and hadn't had the same kind of maturity and self-control that he had now.

At a rap on the door, she startled. But before she could break away, the door flew open, and a woman carrying a baby entered but then stopped abruptly. Her gaze widened upon the two of them, Astrid's body flush against his, her hands fisted in his coat. One of his hands was still in her hair, and the other had ended up on her hip, almost pinning her in place.

The woman peered intently between the two of them. "I guess the rumors are true." The newcomer was petite, her brown hair pulled up in a fashionable style similar to Astrid's, and her pretty face was familiar—one that belonged to Fairplay's midwife.

"Catherine," Astrid said breathlessly, wiggling against him to free herself.

He wasn't ready to release her, guessed he'd never want to let her go if he was really honest about it. But he did the polite thing. He loosened his hold.

Immediately Astrid stumbled backward, cupping her

hands over her cheeks.

He leaned against the doorframe again, crossed his arms, and tried to douse the need that was heating his blood.

"Astrid and Dr. Steele really are getting married." This time Catherine spoke over her shoulder to a man who was playfully wrangling several other children.

Even without the sheriff star on his coat, Dylan McQuaid was easy to recognize with his broad shoulders and muscular frame. The fellow had always been the black sheep of the McQuaid clan, but he'd gotten his life straightened out and now had a wife and a growing family.

Catherine smiled and then began to cross to Astrid. "I knew you'd fall back in love with Logan Steele the second you set eyes on him."

Logan pushed up from the door frame. *Back in love?* Had Astrid once been in love with him? That was a big step beyond the *flame* she'd alluded to last evening with Holt.

He tried to study Astrid's reaction to the words, but Catherine had wrapped Astrid in a one-arm hug.

"Are his kisses as good as the first one he gave you?" Catherine's whisper was soft, but not soft enough.

He'd kissed her? Where and when had that been?

As Astrid broke the embrace from her friend, she didn't look his way and focused on the baby. "And who is this little one?" She spoke hastily, as if she couldn't change the course of the conversation fast enough.

Interesting. His mind scrambled to remember a kiss. Was she referring to the kiss after the barn dance?

He almost snorted. If she thought that kiss had been good, then he needed to show her what *good* really meant.

No. He gave himself a mental kick in the hind quarters. He couldn't allow himself to think that way. Just as when they'd been teenagers, they were parting ways again. And just as then, he couldn't form any attachments, not when he'd only have to break them.

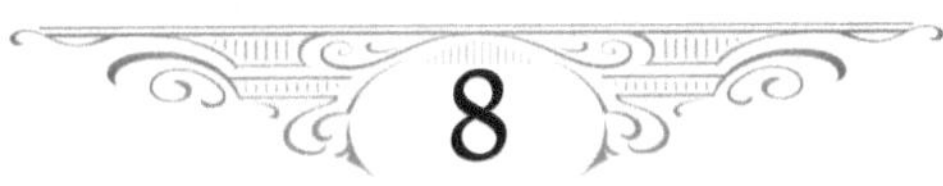

8

Astrid was too flustered to think.

Before she could protest, Catherine and Dylan ushered her and Logan out of the doctor's office into the waiting wagon. Soon, they were on their way to Healing Springs Ranch for a family gathering. Logan sat in the front with Dylan while she reclined in the hay in the back with Catherine and the children.

She needed to clarify with her dear friend what was really going on with Logan and clear up the misunderstanding. But the ride out to the ranch and Greta's enormous house near the inn was filled with too much other chatter, especially with Catherine's children. Austin, her oldest, had been but a baby when Astrid left for Chicago. And now, seeing him so big at six years old and looking just like his pa, a strange despair settled inside.

The feeling came back even stronger when they

arrived at the ranch and she was surrounded by her whole family—all the McQuaid siblings, their spouses, and their many children. Even though she was only twenty-four, a part of her couldn't keep from feeling as if she'd let her life slip past her, that she was turning into an old spinster. If she hadn't left for Chicago, maybe she would have been just like everyone else—married and with babies of her own.

They had supper on the lawn beside the beautiful big white clapboard home that Greta's husband had built for her. They feasted on roasted chicken and numerous fresh vegetables from their large garden, along with pies that Greta had baked.

Astrid ate at a table with the women, thankful she didn't have to sit beside Logan and risk their touching again. Every time she thought about their moment in the waiting room, a fresh flush worked its way through her, and she felt more relieved than ever that Catherine had come in when she had—even if Catherine had blurted embarrassing things about her past relationship with Logan.

He seemed comfortable with the men in her family, joining in on the discussion about the Indian wars in Idaho Territory and a big railroad strike on the Baltimore and Ohio.

After the meal was cleaned up and leftovers stowed away, the men played horseshoes on the lawn, and the women watched from blankets spread on the grass, their conversation centering around their children and babies, as it always seemed to do.

When Catherine had to accompany one of her children to the privy, Astrid offered to hold her newborn daughter.

With the warm bundle pressed against her bosom and the sweet face peering up at her, Astrid's chest squeezed with longing again—longing that had been steadily increasing over the past couple of years. No matter how much she'd tried to ignore it, no matter how often she'd said she would be fine remaining single, no matter how many times she'd reminded herself that her health was too precarious to have a husband and children, the truth was hard to deny in the midst of her big, beautiful family and while holding a baby.

The truth was that she wanted a family and baby of her own. But after so many rejections from would-be suitors, she'd given up hope that any man would ever want to marry a woman doctor. And she'd given up hope that she'd ever have children.

Tears stung Astrid's eyes, and one even managed to escape. She swiped at it and then glanced around to make sure no one had noticed. The other women were too busy chattering, and the men were too occupied with their competition . . . except Logan.

He stood under a tall aspen with the others on his

team. But instead of cheering them on, he was watching her.

Behind him, the mountain sky was painted like a field of wildflowers—lavender and rose and buttercup. Against the backdrop of pale evening light, he looked more handsome than anyone else there. And at home. He'd discarded his hat and coat and rolled up his shirtsleeves. His dark hair was mussed, and the scruff on his jaw lent him a rugged, almost cowboy look.

His brows rose, and his eyes seemed to be asking her if she was okay.

The unruly emotions inside her swirled even faster, and the backs of her eyes smarted again. When was the last time a man had cared how she felt or had paid close enough attention to even notice her feelings?

Logan was a good man.

She gave him a nod and tried for a smile.

He didn't shift his gaze, and his brow only arched more.

Why couldn't a man just like Logan Steele come along and sweep her off her feet? That wasn't too much to wish for, was it?

Dylan smacked Logan on the shoulder with a grin. Logan tossed a comment and smiled back, then started across the grassy yard toward her. As he drew nearer, the conversations of the women tapered into silence, and all eyes focused on her and Logan.

When he halted in front of her, he nodded at the other women before offering his hand to her. "Can we talk for a moment privately?"

Astrid glanced down at the sleeping infant in her arms and then in the direction of the small outhouse beyond the garden. There was no sign of Catherine yet.

Beside her, Greta reached for Catherine's baby. "I'll hold her."

Astrid hesitated. She really shouldn't spend any time alone with Logan, not with how quickly her attraction to him had sprung back to life. But a part of her needed the comfort and understanding of someone who noticed her.

Greta nudged her. "Go on."

How could she resist? Astrid laid the baby in Greta's arms, then took Logan's hand. She'd shed her gloves during the meal and had neglected to put them back on. And Logan was bare-handed as well, so that his warm flesh pressed against hers.

Once she was on her feet, she attempted to slip her hand free, but Logan's fingers closed about hers more securely. "Will you show me that miracle hot spring that healed you?"

She glanced at Greta. "Is that okay? Will there be any guests there?"

Greta seemed to tear her attention away from Logan's hand holding Astrid's and smiled knowingly. "Don't worry. It'll be deserted this time of day." The other women laughed lightly.

Mortification pricked at Astrid. She wasn't asking about the privacy in order to have a tryst with Logan or whatever it was they were imagining. Rather, she'd merely been trying to be polite and not disrupt anyone who might be using the spring.

Logan didn't give her time to clarify and instead tugged her along. The grass muted their steps as they made their way past the inn, which looked like an enormous Southern mansion with four grand columns forming upper and lower balconies framed by elegant cast-iron fences that were painted white. Many of the large windows were open with draperies fluttering in the evening breeze. A few guests lingered on chairs on the wrap-around veranda.

She led Logan toward a path marked by a sign that read "To the hot spring" with an arrow pointing straight ahead through the glittering aspens and few pine trees. She breathed in the scent of sulfur lingering in the air, hoping the properties of the water that had healed her all those years ago would work their powers again so that she'd have many more years ahead.

"I like your family." Logan swung their hands lightly between them.

"Good. Because I like them too."

As they ambled down the path, they talked about each of the McQuaid families, and she updated Logan on the four brothers and one sister along with their spouses and children. All the while, she loved the feel of his fingers, the strength of his hand, the steady shift of his arm.

She cautioned herself not to focus on the awakening feelings too much so that she didn't give way to desires for him that couldn't go anywhere. But at the same time, another thought kept pushing to the forefront of her mind. Was it possible their courtship could move into more?

Even if he'd claimed he didn't want to get married, even if he'd insisted that he was returning to Boston, maybe once he spent time with her and experienced more of their undeniable chemistry, he'd realize they could have a relationship in spite of the obstacles. If they cared enough for each other, surely they could find a way to overcome any barriers that were between them.

Was that only wishful thinking on her part because she was feeling left out of her family with everyone else so happily married?

The guilt of her deception had been nagging her all evening, and she'd been looking for an opportunity to explain to Catherine and Greta—and all the others in her family—that she and Logan weren't really engaged, that in fact, they weren't even courting.

But what if she didn't have to say anything? What if she stopped pretending with Logan and let the current take them where it would?

Did she dare let her interest flare back to life?

As they reached the hot spring and admired the pond, she tugged out of his hold, not quite ready to let her feelings loose. The water was as clear as glass, providing a view of the smooth, glossy pebbles that lined the bottom. Billows of steam rose into the cooler air, droplets glistening on the cattails and willowy grass that grew along the edge.

Over the years, Greta had added a small bathhouse a short distance away and placed a few benches strategically around the pond. Otherwise, she'd kept the sanctuary as natural as possible, letting the beauty and openness of the landscape add to the allure.

Astrid led Logan to one of the benches.

"So, you've missed being here and with your sister?" Logan asked softly. "Is that what is upsetting you tonight?"

She hesitated. Logan had once been a good friend. At the very least, they could be friends again, couldn't they?

"Being with my family reminds me of the solitary life I've carved out for myself." Her admission was hardly more than a whisper. "At gatherings like this, I can't help wondering if I made the right choice to become a doctor at the expense of having my own family."

"You don't think you can have both? Be a doctor and have a family?"

"It's not that I don't think a woman can handle the responsibility of both." She'd read about some of the first women physicians who'd gone on to have husbands and children. "It's that I haven't met a man who appreciates my aspirations."

He was silent for a moment, the laughter and voices of her family wafting their way, the reminder that they couldn't be gone too long. "There are other men like myself who appreciate that women can make fine doctors. I would expect more so here in the West, where many women do men's work."

She hadn't experienced more openness from the men of the West. They all seemed about as stubborn as the men she'd encountered in Chicago. "I thought I'd be alright seeing Catherine with her baby, but I admit, it makes me wish for a baby of my own."

He nodded solemnly. "I can see how being around everyone tonight could stir up longings. It's certainly done that for me. I admit, it's had me wondering if I'm doing the right thing by giving up everything for my career."

"It has?"

"Yes. But then I only need to think of my father." His tone took on a hard note.

She wasn't sure whether his admission made her hopeful or disappointed. Possibly a mingling of both. Was there still a chance that, somewhere inside, Logan harbored hope for a wife and family in his future? Or was he too stubborn to ever allow himself to consider the possibility?

Maybe during the coming days, she could be the one to push him to think about it, since they would apparently be spending a great deal more time together than she'd anticipated. She could at the very least make an effort to win him over . . .

Would jealousy work? She pushed up from the bench and stretched, giving Logan a view of her body—just a small temptation to let him know what he was missing. Sure enough, his sights swept over her, from the arch of her back, to the swell of her chest, and to the length of her throat showing above the neckline of her bodice.

"Once our fake courtship comes to an end"—she brushed at imaginary dust at her waist, drawing his attention there too—"I think I'll send word to Holt to come calling."

"Dolt?" The botched name fell from Logan's lips derisively.

To hide her smile, she started down the path back toward the inn and Greta's house. "He always did have an open mind to my aspirations."

Logan followed on her heels. "That's because he doesn't have all of his brain. His frontal lobe is missing."

She couldn't hold in a chuckle. "At least he'll have me."

"There are better candidates than him."

"Who? Give me specific names."

He listed off several of the more prominent men in town but then just as quickly found fault with each one.

"So, admit it." The worn path was easy to traverse. Ahead, through the foliage, she glimpsed her family still on the lawn. "I have no other option but Holt."

"He wouldn't know what to do with a woman like you." Again the derision in Logan's voice made her smile. Did this ease in riling him up mean that he only needed some persuasion to consider a real relationship? That maybe he wasn't as set against it as he claimed?

As she exited the trail and paused, her body hummed with renewed energy. Maybe it was from breathing in the air at the hot spring. Or what if it was from being with Logan? Somehow, sharing her troubles with him had freed her from her burdens, even if only temporarily.

She braced her hands on her hips and cocked her head at him. "And what does a real man do with a woman like me?"

In two strides he closed the distance between them and dragged her toward him so abruptly that air became trapped in her lungs and her blood ceased pumping. Although he stopped short of pressing their bodies together, the miniscule space between them was so charged she could feel his heat mingling with hers.

His rich dark eyes were drawing her into another hot

pool, beckoning her to wade right in.

Oh, how she wanted to dip her toes into that pool. But she had to maintain the illusion that she still had some control. "Go on," she whispered. "Tell me. If I were yours, what would you do with me?"

His sights dropped to her lips, and his pupils widened, turning his eyes even darker. The pressure of his fingers seared through her skirt and the layers underneath. As his hands tightened, he seemed to be debating whether to close the distance.

She almost leaned in, almost made the first move toward him. But what would happen if she let him kiss her? Would it be the end of this game they seemed to be playing? Would he consider himself to have conquered her and then lose interest? What if that's what had happened with their first kiss?

"Kiss her!" Dylan called with a laugh as more catcalls rang out from the other men.

Fresh embarrassment washed over Astrid at the realization that she and Logan were in plain view of her family. She jerked back, breaking Logan's contact and striding away from him toward the women still lounging on the blanket.

She tensed with each step, half expecting Logan to latch on to her arm from behind, half wanting him to finish what they kept starting . . . or maybe never finished with their first kiss many years ago.

But as she veered toward the women, she could see him heading to the game of horseshoes, grinning and accepting more of the good-natured teasing.

She certainly didn't need him grinning and looking more handsome.

"My stars." In the middle of nursing, Catherine fanned her face with one hand. "Talk about heat."

The other women laughed.

"Oh please." Astrid stepped onto the blanket and sat back in her spot, hoping her face wasn't flaming. "You're exaggerating."

Greta glanced up from a rug she was braiding out of scraps of material. Her smile was tender. "We were just talking about how fast your relationship with Logan has progressed."

"Yes, it's moved quickly." She'd expected the interrogation from her family earlier, so she wasn't surprised the questions were finally coming. "But, with how hastily you jumped into marriage with Wyatt, I figured you'd understand."

"True enough." The thick fabric braid in Greta's hands grew idle as she located her husband among the men and watched him with adoration. "However, just because I had a marriage of convenience doesn't mean that I want you rushing into a relationship."

"I'm old enough to know what I want, Greta." She reached for her sister's hand and patted it. "You don't have to worry about me any longer."

"I admit, I was skeptical when I heard the news of your engagement. I didn't understand how you could be so close to him after just one day back in Fairplay." Greta's tone didn't contain the suspicion that it had earlier in town. "But it's clear from seeing the two of you interact that the sparks are all there."

Here. Now. This was where she needed to admit the truth about her fake courtship and her fake engagement. But as she opened her mouth, the words wouldn't come out.

"Oh yes." Catherine lifted the baby to her shoulder and began a steady thumping against the infant's back. "I could feel that heat the moment I opened the door on them at the doctor's office earlier. But with the way Astrid always talked about him, I suspected she was still in love. And I was right."

In love with Logan? Protest rose in her throat.

Before she could voice it, Catherine spoke again. "I knew that once he took a look at you, he'd be smitten again too."

Their conversation was blessedly cut short by several nieces and nephews converging, calling out questions and complaints.

At least, Astrid *thought* the conversation was over, until Greta leaned in. "I like Logan Steele. I really do. But I'm worried that he'll leave just as soon as his mother dies."

"It's possible." It was more than possible. It was his ultimate goal.

"And if he does, will you go with him?"

"I'm not opposed to it." If she wanted to be with him badly enough, she supposed she'd consider living anywhere just to be with him. But what about him? If her consumption developed further, she'd have no choice but to stay in Colorado. Would he be willing to give up his dreams of living in the East for her?

The real question was whether she could let him do that. And she didn't think she could. Not with how highly he thought of his uncle and the impact their clinic was making in Boston. Certainly not with how excited he'd been about the prestigious lecturing position he'd been given at his college.

As much as she was beginning to desire Logan and wanted to explore the possibility of a future with him, she had to put her feelings for him aside. It was for the best. And it was for the best if they established better boundaries for their fake relationship before it turned real.

9

What was wrong with him that he kept thinking about kissing Astrid?

Logan brushed his hand down the length of Champion's withers. With a chiseled head and a long neck, the dark bay stallion held himself regally, well aware of his power and place in life.

Logan patted the lean body. If only he had as much certainty. Instead, his thoughts had been spinning aimlessly all day. Actually, they'd been spinning since leaving Astrid's side after their walk to the hot spring.

He'd only meant to soothe her hurt after witnessing her tears. But somehow the time alone had turned from compassionate to heated.

Her brothers had teased him to no end about how hungry he was for Astrid. And he hadn't denied it. He still couldn't deny it. But he knew he needed to.

Fading sunshine slanted at just the right angle to

highlight the dust particles rising in the air from the paddock. The fading sunbeams brushed the tips of the pine trees on the foothills beyond Fairplay, turning them to gold. And it glowed against the high mountain peaks, showcasing their granite grandeur.

He had enough time for one hard ride before sunset. And it had been a few days since he'd taken Champion for a run.

"He's a beauty," came a call from the fence closest to the road.

Astrid. He didn't have to turn around to know it was her. Even though they'd parted ways at the office only two hours ago, he couldn't deny that he was eager to see her again, that just the sound of her voice sent a spurt of anticipation through his gut.

Having first gone over to Catherine's house after work, she'd no doubt come so that the two of them could go in and talk to his mother and clarify that they were not engaged. He'd put it off all day, but he'd told Astrid they'd do it together, and he intended to follow through. He wasn't growing more reluctant to do it, was he?

He gave a nod to the groomsman standing in the open barn door at the far end of the paddock. The fellow hustled off, well aware of what Logan was requesting even without words.

Then with a controlled effort, Logan pivoted in Astrid's direction, banking his emotions just as he had during every interaction they'd had throughout the day.

She was astride the gelding that belonged to the Courtney sisters, and she wore the same practical skirt and bodice that she'd had on as they'd worked together, along with a serviceable straw hat with only one ribbon now flapping in the breeze. Even without the finery, she made a fine picture, especially with the way the sunlight fell upon her in soft waves, giving her an ethereal glow.

His mind flashed back to the first time he'd seen her. They'd both been in very similar spots. He'd been inside the paddock with his Arabian mare, and she'd ridden up on a docile horse with one of the Healing Springs cowhands. How old had they been? He couldn't have been much older than eleven, since he'd met her shortly after he'd moved to Fairplay. She must have been ten, just a waif.

Even then, she'd been the prettiest girl he'd ever seen, with her petite frame, big light silvery blue eyes, and fair hair the color of the wheat grass that grew in abundance on the high plains. When she'd stopped to watch him, she'd given him one of her winning smiles, and that's all it had taken for him to be smitten.

She'd gotten down from her horse, climbed into the paddock, and asked him a hundred questions about who he was and where he was from. She hadn't been put off by his sullenness. On her next visit to town, she'd tracked him down in the barn and asked him a hundred more questions.

By the time she'd left, he hadn't felt so alone. She might have been a girl, but he'd known then that he had a friend, one he'd desperately needed.

During the six years he'd lived in Fairplay, her kindness and sweetness had been about the only thing to keep the turmoil inside from raging out of control. The bitterness and anger toward his father had been strong, especially because his father still hadn't spent much time with him or Mother, even after they'd moved to be closer to him.

Gradually, his friendship with Astrid had shifted. He couldn't pinpoint when that had happened or what had caused it. Maybe it had just been inevitable as they'd both matured and gotten older. But during his last year in Fairplay, he'd started noticing changes in the way she'd dressed, in the shape of her body, and in the way she'd held and presented herself.

But he'd also been distracted that last summer before he'd left for the East. He'd argued constantly with his parents about moving back to Boston, had insisted he hated Fairplay, had spoken derisively of the small mountain town. He'd been harsh—and unfair. And after one particularly stressful conversation, he'd threatened to leave and make his own way. His father had finally telegrammed his brother in Boston and made arrangements for college.

The week before leaving to live with Uncle Lloyd,

Logan had wanted to tell Astrid he was going. Even the night of the last dance, he'd known he needed to tell her. But he'd put it off all night, until the end. After it was over, he'd pulled her around the side of the barn to let her know he was moving away. But when she'd peered up at him so expectantly in the faint light of dawn, he'd taken the coward's way out. And he'd kissed her goodbye instead.

It hadn't really been a kiss. More of a peck. But maybe it had meant something to her. And maybe his leaving without ever saying anything had hurt her.

Was that why she'd slapped him in the doctor's office that first day she'd been back?

Something told him he'd finally landed upon the reason for her resentment. And he owed her an apology. One that was long overdue.

"Want to go for a ride with me?" he called.

She peered toward the western range, the sun hovering just behind the bald mountain peaks.

"We have time."

"I don't know—"

"Come on. I want to show you how fast this beauty can run." He smoothed a hand over Champion's mane.

She gave her gelding's neck an affectionate pat. "I'm afraid this old fellow won't be able to keep up."

"We'll ride Champion together."

"Together?" She eyed the stallion appreciatively. She'd

lived among horses and cattle long enough to know quality horseflesh when she saw it. And she'd also learned to ride well and would no doubt relish the power of the Thoroughbred.

The groomsman exited the barn, armed with the stallion's tack.

"No, I can't." She nudged her gelding away from the fence. "We won't both fit in the saddle—"

"Then we'll ride him bareback, bridle and reins only." They would both fit fine in the saddle. In fact, they'd fit mighty fine as far as he was concerned. Nice and tight. But he didn't want to lose this chance to spend time with her outside of their work.

Just as friends. Like they used to be. He could do that, couldn't he?

When she didn't immediately say no, he smiled. "I know you want to."

Her lips lifted into a return smile. "Of course I do."

"You can take the cowgirl out of Colorado, but you can't take the cowgirl out of the girl."

"Maybe."

"No maybe about it. You're a cowgirl through and through."

She didn't deny it. And within the next quarter of an hour, they were atop the Thoroughbred, racing across the grassland. She leaned low against Champion, holding on to his mane. Logan bent low too, pushing the racehorse into a winning gallop.

His thighs gripped the creature hard to stay aloft. And he wound the reins around his leather riding gloves. Though he wasn't squeezed tightly into a saddle behind Astrid, her rounded backside was still brushing against him. His chest pressed against her back, and his arms boxed her in on both sides. The proximity was intoxicating, especially with the powerful pounding of the horse's momentum jarring them together.

He guided the stallion through the flat plains until they reached the wide openness of the sprawling grasslands of South Park, with the Tarryall Range to the east and the Mosquito Range in the west. Dried grass spread out all around them, a few hardy yellow and white wildflowers the only spots of color among the miles of barren earth.

As he halted, he pointed silently to the south to a herd of pronghorns grazing, their bodies blending into the landscape except for their white hindquarters and bulky horns. Astrid watched them silently, the last rays of the setting sun turning the whole grassland into a paradise.

It was at times like this, when the beauty of Colorado overwhelmed him, that he could admit that he didn't mind living there. His memories of Fairplay weren't all bad. The wilderness had a spirit and soul of its own that had a way of taming even the hardest of men. He hadn't realized just how much his life had been shaped by his years in Fairplay until he'd returned to Boston. Only then had he seen the growth, the determination, the fortitude, and other qualities the West had given him.

Although Astrid was keeping a respectable distance from him, for a moment, she seemed to forget about everything else as her gaze swept over the immense landscape. He could feel her relax, not exactly against him, but enough that strands of her hair teased his face.

Now was the perfect opportunity to apologize. He had to do it.

"I should have told you goodbye." He let the words fall without any preamble.

Still holding onto Champion's mane, she twisted.

He braced himself for another slap.

But instead of anger or regrets, her eyes were clear, the amber light of the sun warming her skin and hair to golden honey. "Yes, you should have."

"I have no excuse except that I was young, selfish, and immature."

"I concur."

Again, he couldn't find a trace of malice in her expression. Only frankness. As usual.

"I'm sorry if I hurt you in any way."

This time, she shifted her attention back to the pronghorns, several of them starting to dart away, their white tails flapping, as if to warn of coming danger. "I was young and selfish and immature, too, and I shouldn't have allowed my feelings for you to develop beyond friendship, especially since you never gave me cause to think more could exist."

Her answer should have satisfied him, but instead, a strange unease pricked at him. "My feelings developed more than that too, but I was so ready to leave Colorado."

"And you're ready to leave this time too."

He couldn't deny it.

She was silent several beats.

His muscles tightened. He wanted a friendship with her again. He hadn't realized just how much until this very moment.

"That means friendship is all we can have right now," she hurried to explain. "After last night . . . after my family's assumptions . . . after our closeness, it's in both of our best interests if we keep our fake courtship purely platonic."

A part of him wanted to protest. But he knew she was right.

"That means we need to set some rules for this relationship—boundaries, limits."

"That doesn't sound like any fun." He lightly pushed against her, trying to tease her, but the touch of her body was different now than it had been years ago. Just the slight brush was enough to charge him with keen awareness of her in a way he hadn't had in the past. The rise and fall of her shoulders, the length of her legs near his, and the exposed portion of her neck so fair and so smooth and so tantalizing.

He had to force himself not to look lest he bend in and graze it with his lips.

She set her face forward. "This is a business arrangement between us. We're not supposed to be having fun."

"Friends can have fun."

"But friends don't engage in touching or hugging. And most certainly no kissing. Are we agreed?"

"No."

She stiffened.

"I'm jesting. You're right. And I agree." The problem was, he'd kiss her in a heartbeat if given the opportunity. He'd just have to make sure that didn't happen. "We'll both behave and keep our hands to ourselves. Although I suspect that will be a very big challenge for you."

She elbowed him. "You're incorrigible."

He grinned. "I am. And you like it." Before she could offer a rebuttal or any more rules, he nudged Champion back into motion. As they rode, he relaxed, letting the beauty of the evening and the glory of the ride soothe away all his concerns.

The sky was turning a purplish blue when the barn and paddock came into sight. He wasn't ready for the evening ride to end. He and Astrid had fallen into easy conversation just like they always had, reminiscing about the first time he'd ridden out to Healing Springs Ranch when his Arabian mare had experienced trouble during a birthing. He'd gone out to request the new vet come and help with the foaling, even though the vet had been a woman.

"You always have had a willingness to consider women your equal," Astrid said.

Logan shrugged. "I saw the way my mother had to handle quite a bit after my father left us. She showed me just how strong women can be."

A cowboy riding down the road that led out to the southwest raised his hand in greeting toward them. It was the same road Astrid used to get to the boardinghouse.

At the sight of the man, Astrid stiffened.

"What's wrong?" As soon as Logan uttered the question, he knew what was wrong. The dandy cowboy was Holt, who had apparently intended to ride out to pay Astrid a visit at the boardinghouse.

That low-down, dirty scoundrel. How dare he try to pay a call on Astrid? Not when she wasn't available. Not when they'd made it clear that Astrid was his.

Maybe he was going to have to make it a lot clearer . . .

He brought Champion to a halt near the paddock and wanted to pull her right up onto his lap in a show of possession. But after the rule-making discussion in which he'd agreed to no touching, hugging, or kissing, he couldn't push himself onto Astrid now.

Astrid reached behind him, grabbed his free hand and wrapped it around her middle and at the same time scooted back against him. "Kiss my neck," she whispered.

He couldn't keep his grin from working free. "What about the rules—"

"Forget the rules," she hissed. "Just do it."

He didn't need any further urging to do what he'd been wanting to do the entire ride. He dipped his head and aimed for the tender spot of her neck right beneath her ear, the one that he'd been admiring earlier.

He let his lips graze her skin softly at first, just the merest whisper of a touch, hardly more than just his breath.

She inhaled sharply, and her hand tightened over his at her waist.

She could deny and ignore her physical reaction to him all she wanted, but here was all the proof he needed that she felt the connection between them too. And the proof only rippled through him like the powerful sinews of the horse at full speed.

He dropped his lips again, this time more firmly. The scent of roses lingered on her skin. And she was warm, tasting of sunshine and wind.

Her fingers dug into his arm, and her back pressed further into his chest.

He shifted his mouth to her ear. "You like it. Admit it."

She didn't answer, didn't have time. Holt was drawing near, his wide eyes taking in their cozy riding arrangement.

The rugged cowboy had obviously cleaned himself up, shaved, and changed into fresh clothing for his trip out to visit Astrid. But hopefully, the message was now clear. Astrid wasn't interested in him and didn't want him back.

"Dagnabbit." Holt pulled back on the reins of his mount, causing the creature to sidestep. "I thought you were playing with me the other night. But looks like I was wrong."

"Why would I be playing with you, Holt?" Astrid held on to Logan's arm, but her grip now wasn't one of passion. It had quickly shifted into one filled with all her hurts and fears.

"Oh, you know." Holt offered a sheepish grin. "Everyone I talked to said your engagement to Logan couldn't be real, that it happened too fast. So I reckoned you were just trying to make me jealous."

Logan snorted. The fellow thought a lot of himself to assume Astrid was faking an engagement to make him jealous—even if it was true.

"Another alternative is quite possible." Her tone was cold.

"What's that, darlin'?" Holt's grin made a quick appearance. And Logan could see why the cowboy had captured Astrid's affection. He could be a handsome and charming man when he put his mind to it.

"That alternative is that I truly do not care about you anymore, Holt, and that I got over you long ago."

Holt's grin fell away, and his horse took another quick step back. "When Logan runs off again, I'll be here waiting for you." He shot Logan a hard look before focusing on Astrid again. "You know I ain't going nowhere. Unlike the fancy doctor here."

Logan wanted to offer a rebuttal, but how could he? He *was* leaving again. That was the truth. He hadn't hidden that fact from anyone. Everyone in Fairplay knew he'd only come to take care of his mother and didn't intend to practice in the small mountain community forever.

In a couple of months, Astrid would pretend to break up with him. And then would she seek out Holt?

The prospect was as unsettling today as it had been last night during their conversation at the hot spring.

Holt gave her a nod before turning his horse around, clicking his tongue, and setting out at a fast trot.

Astrid watched the man ride away for several heartbeats before sitting forward. "Blast," she whispered. "What have I done?"

"I think you've made it impossible for us to tell my mother that we're not engaged." Logan tried to manufacture frustration, but strangely, the only emotion he felt was relief.

She sighed, then she twisted, clearly trying to break free of his hold.

He released her and slid down from the horse.

As much as he relished the physical attraction with Astrid, which was abundantly alive and well, he had to stick with their agreement to have boundaries, even when she was the one climbing over the fence and breaking all the rules.

She might be the one starting blazes, but he was mature enough to stomp them out.

The truth was, as much as he liked fire, it was dangerous. He needed to be careful or they would both get burned.

10

The screaming lad had finally fallen unconscious, even before they'd been able to administer ether. The examining room had grown quiet except for the few instructions Logan had exchanged with Astrid.

With how mangled the boy's finger was, Logan had appreciated having an assistant, especially one so proficient. As usual, Astrid had proven to be calm and sharp-minded during the crisis.

"I think I have the last of the bone fragments." Peering through the magnifying glass he was holding for her, she lowered the sterilized tweezers into the tendons and flesh of the boy's hand and plucked out another sliver before dropping it into the dish beside her.

He picked up the scalpel and held it out to her. "You may as well finish."

"No. You do it." She glanced at the lad's father, a thin Chinese man standing near the door, his solemn eyes white amidst the grime on his face. Beyond him in the waiting room were a couple other men from the mine, their faces and clothing covered in dark dust, the same as the lad's.

Only ten, the boy had been trembling with shock and pain when the men had rushed him in, his finger having been crushed under a cart's wheel in Steele's Mine, one of the only functioning mines left in Fairplay since the gold rush had started back in '59.

The mine had made his father a very wealthy man, and instead of taking his wealth and returning to the East as he'd claimed he would do, Father had invested more into his mine, developing the equipment and manpower to make the mining operations sustainable. While it wasn't pulling out extraordinary amounts of gold anymore, it was still doing well.

Why his father was allowing the mine's foreman to hire boys this young, Logan didn't know and could only shake his head in frustration.

"Please. Do not cut off hand," the father pleaded with a thick Chinese accent.

There wasn't any need to do something that drastic—unless, of course, infection set in.

"We won't. Just the finger." Logan tried to pass the scalpel again to Astrid. This time she took it, although hesitantly, again glancing at the father for his reaction.

The man gave a slight bow, as though giving Astrid

permission to do the surgery.

She nodded in return. Then without blinking an eye, she sliced the sharp blade through the exposed digital nerve and torn skin. With how crushed the boy's bone had been, there was no need for the sturdier instruments that were sometimes necessary to saw through muscle and bone.

An instant later the deed was done. She passed the scalpel back to him and then took his offering of needle and catgut before bending close to the stump and starting the intricate work of suturing the flesh.

She worked silently and efficiently, her delicate fingers coated in blood but undeterred in her mission.

A thrill wound through Logan as it had many times over the past few days that she'd labored alongside him. From abscesses to apoplexy and from boils to bloody flux, she'd approached each patient without any squeamishness. Not only that, but her diagnoses had been accurate, her treatments had been modern, and her compassion for the patients had been unmatched.

If she were a man, he would have handed the medical practice over to her in a heartbeat. As word of her expertise spread, women and children were beginning to request her services. In fact, the women seemed to like having a female doctor who understood their feminine issues.

However, most of the fellows still scoffed at her.

Logan suspected they were embarrassed to have a woman as beautiful as Astrid see them in any state of undress or at their worst.

Besides, the more he was with Astrid, the more he disliked the idea of her tending to half-naked men. He didn't want them making lurid comments as if she were no better than a saloon dancer.

With her head bent, she focused so intently—as she always did—that he had the freedom to study her face without her being aware—the wrinkles in her forehead, the strands of hair plastered to her temple, and her delicate eyebrows.

He wanted to take his thumb and smooth out the worry. But the truth was, he couldn't keep touching her and remain sane. He'd realized that after kissing her neck during their ride on Champion earlier in the week. The taste and texture of her had lingered with him the rest of the night and next day.

Even now, every time he caught a glimpse of her bare neck, he imagined bending down and kissing her there again.

That's why the rest of the week, he'd taken extra care not to get too near to her or to be alone with her. And she'd seemed to be doing the same, as though she recognized that they were better off keeping some distance. She'd apologized for asking him to pretend around Holt, had vowed she wouldn't do it again.

Although he'd used extreme self-control around her all week, he found that he was drawn to her more every day. He supposed it was inevitable after the hours they spent together in the office and making house calls. Only one afternoon had he gone by himself, leaving her to tend to patients in the clinic without him. And of course, he hadn't involved her in any nighttime emergencies.

"There." She snipped the last thread, examined the wound again, then reached for a towel and started to wipe her hands. She glanced at the clock on his writing table, then straightened. "Oh dear. Is it after five already?"

"It's not terribly late—"

"It's late if I'm to be at your mother's party on time." She finished wiping her hands and then began to gather the bloody instruments.

Logan took the items from her. "I'll take care of everything. You need to go."

She hesitated, looking first to the lad and then his father.

"I'll give them final instructions and some opium for the pain."

"You're sure?" She was already untying the apron that she wore over her garments.

"We can't disappoint my mother, can we?"

Astrid just shook her head. Like him, she'd obviously given up on trying to clarify the nature of their relationship not only to his mother but to everyone. Once the invitations to the engagement party had gone out to the town as well as the surrounding area, they'd both known it would be impossible to retract the news.

Although Logan had made a concerted effort to explain again to his mother that he and Astrid weren't officially engaged, she'd only insisted that it didn't matter, that an official proposal wasn't necessary to celebrate.

Even though Mother was getting weaker every day, talking about his engagement and planning the party seemed to have given her renewed purpose and energy. When he'd explained that to Astrid, she'd finally stopped pestering him to have his mother cancel the party.

"You'll still be able to break up with me just as easily whether we're courting or engaged," he'd told her. "Besides, nothing has to change between us just because people believe we're engaged."

They'd attend the party tonight, tomorrow they'd sit together in church, and then on Monday they'd go back to being nothing but fellow physicians fighting against disease and death in the community.

Within minutes, Astrid was out the door and on her way to the livery to collect her horse and ride to the boardinghouse. Logan finished tending to the lad, sent everyone on their way, and hastily cleaned up from the surgery.

As he made his way down Main Street toward his family's home, he could hardly go a dozen feet without someone stopping him, either to talk about the party or to ask for advice about an ailment. When he finally made it to the trellised walkway, the yard was busy with what looked like an army of servants decorating, setting tables, arranging food, and more. Delicious smells of a dozen different delicacies wafted in the air.

"Logan." His father strode from among the chaos. Attired in his best black suit and a top hat, he made a dashing figure. His face was lean with a neatly trimmed beard and mustache, both threaded with silver, and his eyes were deep-set and dark, framed by equally dark brows.

People often remarked how much Logan looked and acted like his father. Although he'd always hated the comparison, he'd accepted it.

While many similarities were unavoidable, there was one thing he could control. He refused to disappoint and fail a woman the way his father had disappointed and failed his mother. Logan could still picture her weeping the day his father had walked out the door. Her sobs had torn at Logan's heart then and after each of his father's subsequent visits home over the years.

But her pleas and ultimatums hadn't softened Father's heart. He'd done whatever he'd wanted without any consideration to the wife and son he'd left behind. Finally Mother had no choice but to uproot her life and move to Fairplay, but even then Father had been too busy running the town and his mine and all his other businesses to cherish Mother.

Father's newest venture as state senator was exactly the kind of ambition that he'd always had and was now taking him away again, this time to Denver for long weeks at a time. Even though Father rode up to Fairplay as often as he could, Logan could only shake his head in disgust that the man had even taken the political office. He'd known at that point Mother had uterine cancer. He'd also known the prognosis wasn't fabulous. But he'd valued his prestige and power more than her—as usual.

"There you are." His father crossed the lawn toward him. "You're late and worrying your mother."

The words sliced into Logan like a sharp scalpel. How dare his father say anything about being late and worrying Mother? After his years of absence and busyness, he had no right to criticize anyone else.

Logan wanted to keep walking toward the front veranda and ignore his father altogether. But he'd been too well trained to disrespect his father and had learned to fume privately instead.

His father held out a hand for a handshake.

Logan stopped and took it. "Father. How was your trip up?"

"No bandits attacked the stage." Even though his father joked about bandits, he'd been on the same stagecoach that had brought Astrid and Greta to Fairplay many years ago, one that had been robbed by a gang of thieves.

His father's grasp was strong and his eyes warm. "I was glad to get the telegram from your mother regarding your engagement. I'd begun to despair that you'd never settle down."

A terrible urge to contradict the man prodded Logan. He wanted to blurt out that he wasn't engaged and didn't have plans to settle down. And that he didn't care if his father was glad or not.

But he held his words in check. Mostly. "I'm doing this for Mother."

His father released his hand and clamped his shoulder instead. "She looks really happy—happier than she's been in a long time."

If the man had spent more time with his wife, maybe she would have been happier before this week. But it was too late for that. "She's enjoyed planning the party."

"I can see that. She seems to have more energy and color than when I was last home."

How long had it been since his father's last trip home? Two weeks? A month? "The distraction has been good for her."

His father's brows drew together, and a haggardness fell over his features. "Give me your honest opinion, Logan. How much time does she have left?"

"A month. Maybe two at the most."

At the blunt words, Father flinched. "Maybe all this excitement will give her the needed energy to keep fighting."

Logan hoped so. He didn't want to see her suffer from pain or debilitation, but he wasn't ready to let her go. Wasn't sure that he'd ever be ready to lose her.

A call from his mother floated through the open front window.

"You'd better get on in there." His father backed up a step. "You've kept her waiting long enough."

Logan's muscles tightened. *He'd* kept her waiting long enough? He'd been there for her every day. He'd sacrificed his career and ambitions in the East to live with her during her last days. He'd even given in to her obsessive need for him to find a woman.

And where had his father been for the majority of the time? And what sacrifices had Senator Steele made for his wife?

None.

Logan gave his father a curt nod and started down the path again to the house.

As soon as Mother passed away, Logan would put as much distance as possible between himself and the man. In fact, if he never had to see his father again, that would be alright with him.

11

Astrid couldn't stop fidgeting with her gown, straightening and shifting the layers of ruffles. The vibrant blue taffeta was her best color, and she'd purposefully chosen it to make her eyes bluer.

Driving the wagon beside her, Charity cast her a glance. "You're nervous."

Astrid clasped her hands in her lap and tried to ignore the flock of finches flapping around in her stomach as the outline of Fairplay came into view. "A little. Thank you for coming with me."

"I admit I'm nervous too." Charity smoothed a hand over her skirt—her Sunday best, but certainly much plainer and duller than anything Astrid owned. Even with the simple attire, Charity was still beautiful with her red hair hanging in long waves, her figure perfect and curvy even without a corset.

When Astrid had raced home to get ready for the

party, Charity had offered to help. In the process, Astrid had learned that the young woman had never gone to a party before. Having grown up in a strict and pious Quaker community, their socials had been simple affairs.

Astrid had convinced Charity to come along, suggesting that if she mingled more and got to know the townsfolk, she'd have a better chance of gaining business at the boardinghouse.

After the past week of living with the Courtney sisters, Astrid had grown fond of them. They were gracious and kind and accommodating. And they deserved more boarders. But whenever Astrid explained to patients and others around town where she was living, she quickly surmised that most people were mistrustful of the girls' Quaker background, even though the girls hadn't been practicing Quakers since before their parents died a year and a half ago, had apparently had a falling away from their Quaker community, and had come to the West wanting to start over.

Astrid reached across the bench and squeezed Charity's hand. "You're going to steal the attention of every eligible man tonight."

Charity's lips curled into a smile, one that showed her pleasure at the compliment. "You'll be the center of attention."

"Mark my word, you'll gain more suitors than you'll know what to do with."

Charity laughed lightly, a sweet tinkling. "I don't need suitors, Astrid. I have a boardinghouse to run and my sisters to care for."

"I'm sure you can make room in your life if the right man comes along."

"Like you're doing?"

After the past week of facing a hundred questions from people around town—old friends and acquaintances, and even complete strangers who were curious about Doctor Steele's *woman*—she'd thought the pretending would get easier. But guilt still pricked at her.

Most of the time she'd assuaged her conscience by telling herself that the relationship wasn't entirely made up. She'd always liked Logan, and he was even easier to like now as a man. If their circumstances had been different—if she didn't have the worry of consumption and he didn't have such remarkable opportunities back East—maybe they could have made things work.

"Logan is a wonderful man." She bit back a sigh at the many ways he'd proven that over the past week of working together. She couldn't even begin to list all the things she liked about being his partner. The surgery on the boy this afternoon was the perfect example of how humble he was to allow her to do the amputation while he acted as the assistant. And even when he was the one doing the procedure, he involved her in every aspect.

The week had flown by. Mostly they'd treated the

usual issues: ingrown toenails, goiters, a mild case of erysipelas, earaches, and a case of syphilis. Surely he had to see they worked well together. If only he wanted to stay . . .

But earlier today, he'd posted additional advertisements for a partner in more newspapers. He hadn't told her he was doing so, but she'd peeked at him through the window of the waiting room as he'd entered the post office, and later when she'd gone to check on her mail, she'd discretely learned about the telegrams Logan had sent to several large city newspapers.

"It's easy to see how much you adore him." Charity focused ahead on the other wagons and carriages parked in the field across from the Steeles' home.

Astrid wanted to deny Charity's statement, but what good would come of doing so? "Yes, Logan Steele is an easy man to adore."

It wouldn't be difficult to act the part of adoring fiancée tonight. At the very least, she'd have no trouble convincing Mrs. Steele that she cared about Logan. Hopefully with the display, Mrs. Steele would be satisfied with how things were progressing and would cease meddling in her and Logan's lives.

Already a crowd had gathered on the spacious back lawn among the tents that had been erected. Clipped hedges and raised flower gardens gave the yard the look of a grand English estate. Some of the guests were playing croquet and lawn bowls. Others were admiring the horses in the paddock.

Astrid's gaze went directly to Logan near the house. He was attired in an evening suit with a formal black tailcoat, a matching double-breasted waistcoat, white shirt and bow tie, and black trousers. He was darkly handsome and stood out from everyone else, as usual—always the most dashing man present.

Charity slowed her wagon to a stop. As a valet approached, Logan's sights landed upon them as if he'd been watching and waiting for her. He spoke a few more words to the gentlemen surrounding him, likely excusing himself, before striding toward the wagon.

With his dashing smile, he assisted them both down and then led them around, introducing them and giving them a chance to mingle. He seemed relaxed, but stiffened when his father strolled around the house, pushing Mrs. Steele in her chair with wheels. In spite of how sick the woman was, she looked elegant in her silk evening gown in the new princess-line style, her hair fashionably coiled with pearl-studded combs.

She took her place in a lounge chair positioned under one of the canopies, with Mr. Steele standing beside her. Astrid let Logan guide her gradually toward his parents, until at last, he helped situate her into the chair next to his mother, then took his place standing at her side.

Astrid exchanged pleasantries with Logan's parents for

several moments as servants began to dispense drinks and hors d'oeuvres. She'd only just begun to relax and sensed Logan's stiffness dissipating when Mr. Steele called out over the gathering that his wife had a few words she wanted to say.

By now, the crowd had swelled, and Astrid could see her family among the guests. She wasn't sure where Charity had gone off to but hoped the young woman was having a good time.

"Welcome, everyone." The joy in Mrs. Steele's expression rivaled the sun that was still warm in the July evening. "We're so happy to have you here tonight to celebrate our wonderful son's engagement to this lovely young woman."

Mrs. Steele reached for Astrid's hand and patted it while bestowing on her a grateful smile, as if Astrid were responsible for single-handedly wrangling Logan out of his life of bachelorhood. Astrid prayed the dear woman would never learn the truth about their deception. It would likely kill her.

"I've been informed by both my son and future daughter-in-law that the engagement isn't official." Mrs. Steele paused and nodded at her husband. He dipped his hand into his inner coat pocket and pulled out a small black velvet box. With a flourishing bow, he presented it to Logan.

Logan's eyes widened enough for Astrid to know he'd

had no part in this plan his parents had orchestrated. He opened the box and then shot Astrid an apologetic look.

Oh dear. What was Mrs. Steele up to now?

"There you are, Logan." Mrs. Steele beamed up at her son. "Now, go ahead and do this right and make me proud."

Logan's jaw ticked as he took in his parents' faces and then surveyed the people gathering closer and watching with unfettered excitement.

Logan hesitated only a moment longer before lowering himself to one knee before Astrid, his dark gaze filling with angst. Even so, he had the most gorgeous eyes of any person who'd ever lived. Especially when he was serious, as he was now. The dark brown turned soulful and solemn, a combination that never failed to make her want to wrap him into an embrace and promise him that everything would turn out fine.

As his attention once again returned to the velvet box, her sights dropped to it as well. There, nestled against the black, was a shiny gold band graced with a simple blue sapphire in the center. He lifted it out, and as he did so, he met her gaze again. "Will you marry me, Astrid? One word from you will make me the happiest man in the universe."

He was asking as politely as any gentleman would, using the formal verbiage many men used for proposals. And the ring was certainly one of the most beautiful a bride-to-be could ask for. If only he meant his words. If only one word from her truly would make him the happiest man in the universe.

His eyes pleaded with her to do this, and she knew she couldn't refuse. They were in too deep now to do anything but keep the charade going.

She curved her lips into a practiced smile, one she'd perfected long ago. "Yes. Of course I'll marry you."

As the crowd clapped, the tension in his features eased, and he lifted the ring.

She quickly tugged off her glove and offered him her hand.

As his fingers closed around hers, he began to slide the ring on. Slowly. Caressing her with each inch. As though he was revering her.

When the ring was finally situated, her body was taut, ready for more. But what?

He didn't release her hand. Instead, he brought it to his lips. And though he'd kissed her hand the night she'd come for supper with his mother, she'd had her gloves on, and the gesture had been polite, nothing more.

But now, as he pressed his lips to her bare skin, the warmth and solidity of his lips only made her think of the kiss upon her neck when they'd been riding the Thoroughbred and had come upon Holt. Even though the brush of his lips had been brief, it had been so delectable that she'd dreamed about it almost every night since then.

What would it be like to have him kiss her again, this time on her lips?

As he raised his head, she couldn't stop from watching his mouth, cataloging each curve, indentation, line, and even the slightly plumper bottom lip. When those lips began to stretch into a cocky grin, she guessed he'd figured out the direction of her thoughts and was amused by her fascination.

She jerked her attention away from him and settled it on his mother, who was dabbing tears from the corners of her eyes with a handkerchief.

Logan rose gracefully to his feet, then offered a hand to help Astrid up. She didn't have the chance to put her glove on, supposed she would need to keep it off in order to show people her ring. But again, as he captured her hand, he caressed her, almost as if he relished the feel of her, too, and couldn't get enough.

She stood beside him, a strange lightness making her feel as though she were floating, airless, breathless. She needed to focus on the guests and this very public engagement, didn't want anyone to realize she'd just been thinking about Logan's mouth.

As Logan slanted a glance her way, his sights dropped to her lips, almost as if she'd beckoned him to look there with her wayward thoughts. His attention lingered, and something flared in his dark eyes.

"The two of you need to seal your engagement with a

kiss." Mrs. Steele's voice rang out loud and certain. For a woman who was weak and sick, she could certainly project herself.

"Dash it, Mother," Logan whispered a side mumble. "Not here. Not in front of everyone."

"Nonsense. Everyone would love to see you give your bride-to-be a kiss." Mrs. Steele peered out over the smiling faces. "Wouldn't you all?"

The group called out affirmations followed by cheers and whistles.

Logan exhaled noisily.

"Kiss her!" The shout came from Dylan at the outer edge of the crowd, his arm around Catherine. He was instigating them. Again.

Astrid wanted to tell him to wipe the silly grin from his face. At the very least, she would have a stern talk with him later and tell him about the need to mind his own business.

In the meantime, what else could she and Logan do except kiss?

If they refused, people might question the authenticity of their relationship. They didn't want to chance that, did they? And they couldn't risk hurting Mrs. Steele and causing her a setback.

Logan was already pivoting toward her, likely coming to the same conclusions. They would have to kiss in order to make everyone—especially his mother—happy. But they could do this. They'd do nothing more than brush lips. Short. Simple. And to the point.

She shifted so that she was facing him now too, offering him what she hoped was a reassuring smile. They could get through this. It didn't have to be an ordeal.

Logan didn't smile in return. Instead, he stepped against her so that his chest brushed hers.

She sucked in a swift breath, but before she could gain her bearing, he dipped down and caught her mouth. She'd expected tentativeness and tenderness, like the first time those many years ago. But his captivity was powerful and thorough. He moved with the expertise and boldness of a skilled explorer who knew his destination and intended to take her there with him.

For the first moment, she let him guide her through the unfamiliar but beautiful terrain, too surprised and too swept up by the strength of his kiss to respond. But his urging pushed her to open up, let him in, and to take the journey with him.

Oh, please. She wanted to go—would go anywhere with him, would even scale a mountain. For a moment, the kiss transported her away from the engagement party and to the highest peak, where they were together without anyone else, their lips tangling, their breaths mingling, and their hearts beating as one.

But the clapping from the crowd told her everyone was satisfied with the effort. She and Logan were done.

She broke away, her lips tingling and warm and damp. Her cheeks, her neck, her chest were overheating, and she wanted to slip her fan out of her reticule and pump air against herself. But doing so would only signal to everyone just how much Logan's kiss had seared her. And it had seared her body, soul, and very existence.

He didn't move for the span of several heartbeats. What was he thinking?

More importantly, what had she done? Had she really passionately kissed Logan Steele in front of half the town?

"That was just beautiful." Mrs. Steele blotted the corners of her eyes once more. "It's so wonderful to see young love."

Astrid didn't dare glance at Logan. She was afraid to see his reaction, to find that maybe he was panicking. After all, a public engagement followed by a public kiss wasn't what either of them had bargained for.

She could admit panic was the farthest thing from her mind. Her swirling thoughts kept landing on the fact that he'd kissed her. Passionately. And every single second of it had been glorious.

"With such a beautiful engagement," Mrs. Steele continued, "there's really only one thing left to do." She held out both of her frail hands, one toward Logan and one to Astrid.

As Logan placed his hand in his mother's, Astrid did the same.

The matron immediately brought their two hands together, forcing Logan to intertwine his fingers through Astrid's before wrapping both of hers around them. "The only thing left to do is set the wedding date."

A spurt of anxiety shot through Astrid. Mrs. Steele couldn't be serious, could she?

"I say as soon as possible so that I can be a part of the beautiful occasion."

Astrid almost choked. As soon as possible? What exactly did that mean?

Mrs. Steele looked up at her husband still standing beside her. "What do you think, Landry?"

"Whatever you wish, darling." He patted her shoulder gently, his expression filled with understanding.

"Four weeks? No, three. That ought to give me enough time to plan a wedding." Mrs. Steele smiled at Logan. "What do you say?"

He tucked a finger into his collar and tugged at it.

How could they deny his mother the opportunity to be a part of their wedding before she passed away? And yet, how could they agree to a wedding date for a fake engagement? They had to set a limit somewhere.

"Mother," Logan started but then cleared his throat as if the very mention of marrying in three weeks had put an invisible noose around his neck. "It is rather soon."

"But I'd like it to be soon so that I can still enjoy the day." Mrs. Steele was still holding their hands together, and the entire crowd was silent, intently watching the interaction. "If we wait a month or two, I might be too sick by then to participate."

Logan hesitated. "Astrid and I have just been reunited. We were hoping to spend more time together before getting married."

"Nonsense." His mother patted their hands a final time before releasing them. "You'll have your whole lives to spend time together. But you'll only have me for a couple more months."

Astrid wanted to jump into the conversation and bring an end to the discussion. All they had to do was confess to everyone that their relationship was a charade.

With fingers still intertwined, Logan squeezed her hand, drawing her gaze. His eyes pleaded with her not to make the confession, almost as if he'd realized the direction of her thoughts.

"What do you say, Astrid?" Mrs. Steele asked. "Are you willing to give a dying woman her greatest wish? To see her son happily married?"

Astrid swallowed every last word of protest. How could she deny such a heartfelt request? Especially here and now with everyone looking on so expectantly.

"Of course." Astrid forced cheer to her words. "Three weeks until the wedding should be just fine."

She couldn't. She'd have to wait until later, after the party, to tell Mrs. Steele no. She and Logan might have a fake relationship and a fake engagement, but a fake wedding? That would be taking things too far.

12

Logan twirled the steps of the dance, much too aware of Astrid's every move, every breath, every word.

Even though he was working hard at keeping his mind from going back to the kiss he'd given her earlier in the evening, he'd replayed the moment at least a hundred times over the past several hours of visiting with guests. The tangle of their lips had been explosive, bringing a surge of desire he hadn't expected. Desire for more of her. Desire to hold her again. Desire to explore what the passion could be like between them.

As much as he wanted to explore, he couldn't. He had to keep up the stiff wall of self-control, for his own sanity. If he didn't, he'd easily find himself drowning in her.

With the fading sunset lingering on the western mountain range and darkness settling around the yard, lanterns had been lit, a blazing bonfire crackled in a fire pit, and the orchestra was playing.

Even though his mother had retired to her room—with his father—and was no longer policing his every move and ensuring he was by Astrid's side every single second, he'd known he had to finish out the party by dancing with Astrid. If he didn't, his mother would hear about it and be disappointed. Besides, it was the right thing to do.

He'd excused himself from the men smoking cigars and had interrupted her conversation with the ladies to ask her to dance. Of course, she'd acquiesced, having played her role as his fiancée to perfection. In fact, she'd done her part above and beyond what he'd initially asked of her when they'd made their agreement.

How could he ever begin to repay her for going along with everything? Especially with the party and the kiss and now dancing. He would owe her much more than a place in the partnership.

A part of him felt guilty for having made the bargain for the partnership. But another part wasn't the least remorseful for getting the chance to be with her like this.

Thus far throughout the dancing, he'd kept her a respectable distance away, holding one of her hands up between them while keeping his other hand upon her waist. And her curvaceous hip. If he spread his fingers, he'd all too easily give himself a tour of her stomach and her ribs—which he didn't intend to do. Not at all.

He bent his head closer to her hair and drew in a

breath of her floral scent. The headiness of it sent a tremor of fresh need through him. And he couldn't keep his fingers from tightening on her hip.

She resituated her grip around his bicep, her fingers trembling as she did so.

Had she felt his need? Did she feel the same? Or was she nervous?

His muscles tensed. What in the deuce was he doing? Even if she were feeling half of what he was, their relationship couldn't go anywhere, could it? Not when their lives were headed in two different directions. And they'd already decided friendship was all they could offer each other.

He had to reassure her that he wouldn't act on his attraction again, that she was safe with him, and that he'd find a way to make his mother understand that he didn't intend to get married in three weeks.

"Astrid?" he whispered.

"Hmmm . . .?" She had yet to look directly into his eyes since their kiss and was staring at his tie and his high starched collar.

He leaned in farther to speak privately for her ear alone. "I'm sorry for everything getting out of hand tonight."

"Your mother is one determined lady."

"Yes, she is."

Astrid was close enough that he could feel her soft

exhalations. He wanted to move his mouth near hers and let those respirations mingle with his. But he closed his eyes and blocked out the picture that was rapidly forming in his mind of pressing against her and giving himself permission to taste and try and tease her lips until she responded again as she had earlier with a hunger that rivaled his.

"I feel bad, Logan." Her whisper was low and against his neck.

"Don't." Somehow his feet kept moving to the steps of the dance, having practiced enough to keep time with the music even though his mind was fully tuned in to Astrid and nothing else. "We'll get through tonight. Then tomorrow, I'll make clear that three weeks is too soon."

"She'll just pressure us for four. And we won't be able to tell her no." Astrid's fingers again trembled against his arm.

"I can tell her no."

She released a soft scoffing sound. "Your inability to say no to her is exactly why we're in this predicament."

A denial pushed at the forefront of his thoughts, but he bit it back. Astrid was right. If he'd had more fortitude with his mother, he would have been firm from the start of her matchmaking.

"I'm sorry." Her whisper filled with remorse. "That wasn't fair to place the blame on you when it's my fault for persisting in the engagement to make Holt jealous."

"Even so, I should have made it clear that we weren't considering marriage."

"I could have made it clear to her too."

"I'll tell her we're waiting a year."

"And do you really think she'll go along with that?"

"She'll have to."

He'd guided them away from the other dancers, leaving the ring of light the lanterns provided, giving them more privacy. The grass beneath their feet was longer and drier and crunched with each twirl. Away from the heat of the bonfire, the chill of the coming night cooled his overheated skin.

"Your mother has gone to a lot of trouble to orchestrate us being together." Astrid's comment once again held chagrin. "I'll feel terrible disappointing her."

It was his turn to scoff. "What are you saying? That we should go through with the marriage in three weeks just so that we keep her happy?"

She didn't immediately deny his ludicrous suggestion.

At her pause, his heartbeat picked up pace. She wasn't really considering marrying him, was she?

He hadn't given himself permission to consider marriage in so long that he shook his head and threw out the idea.

"If it makes her happy, should we consider it?" Her voice was soft, even shy.

His dance steps faltered. Did Astrid want to get married?

During their walk to the hot spring that night at her sister's place, she'd mentioned how she was sad because she didn't have a family of her own, that there were so few men who wanted her because they couldn't appreciate that she was a doctor.

What if he could be that man? He definitely wanted her. There was no sense in denying that. And he could most certainly appreciate her skills as a doctor.

But marry her?

No. He couldn't.

He almost shook his head, but he didn't want to hurt her, didn't want her to think that he was like the other men who'd rejected her.

"Never mind." Her tone held mortification. She'd obviously sensed his reticence, guessed his lack of response meant that he didn't like the idea. "You told me you didn't want to get married. Why would that change?"

He wasn't sure why it would change, only that if anyone could make him rethink his plans, she was the one. "Maybe because I met you."

It was true. He'd never known a woman like Astrid. He'd always assumed that being a doctor would prevent him from spending time with his wife. But with Astrid, their careers actually brought them together more. Maybe he wouldn't have to sacrifice his ambitions after all. He could have a wife and do all the other things he wanted without worry about neglecting anyone. If they eventually had children, they'd have to figure out how to juggle everything. But it was certainly worth considering, wasn't it?

"We met a long time ago, Logan."

"And we've always liked each other." He may as well admit what they already knew. "We still do."

She swayed to the music, still staring at his bow tie. He waited for her to agree with him, but she only captured her bottom lip between her teeth.

The motion sent swift heat through his gut—heat he didn't need at the moment if he wanted to think with a level head. "It's clear after the past week that we make a good team."

"We do . . ."

"But . . ."

"But you have a life waiting for you in the East. And I have a new life waiting for me here."

"I'm sure we can work it out." He had no doubt his uncle would allow her to work at the clinic. And surely their women patients would accept her.

But could he really take a wife? He'd kept the possibility out of reach for so long that he wasn't sure he could give himself permission to finally consider it.

Before he could stop himself, he lowered his head so that his lips brushed against the stretch of neck right by her ear, the same place he'd kissed her while on Champion. Heaven, have mercy. Her skin was as soft as a rose petal just unfurling. He breathed her in, inhaling her and wishing he could only and ever breathe her.

Her dancing steps came to a halt.

Deuces. He'd moved too fast. Was too eager for her. He had to be careful, or he'd scare her away. "I apologize—"

Her hand slipped from his bicep, and she clutched his vest, as if to keep him from moving back.

He stilled. Maybe she was just as eager for him as he was for her. And the very prospect of her eagerness drove desire through him like the strike of flint against stone.

He dipped back in and let his lips hover beneath her ear. He needed to take another taste of her, and nothing would stop him. As he let his mouth make contact with the silky warmth, her breath caught with a soft gasp that struck the flint inside him again, even harder.

Her chest rose quickly, and as much as he wanted to keep from looking, his gaze dropped to her curves, a slight pale swell all that showed at her neckline past the ruffles.

"Watch that hankering, Dr. Steele," came the voice of one of the McQuaid men.

Astrid broke away first, just as she had with their kiss earlier.

Logan shifted his gaze to find that they had an audience. At some point the orchestra number had come to an end, and the other dancers had stopped. Now every person was staring at them, had seen him kissing Astrid. Again.

"Three weeks," said another of the McQuaids. "You've got three weeks until the wedding. Until then . . ."

Guffaws and titters echoed around them. But he found himself finally looking into Astrid's silver-blue eyes, glittering with a beauty that rivaled the stars.

Should he give marriage to her more serious consideration?

Her eyes and expression wavered with doubt.

As much as she seemed to like him, was something holding her back?

He had the urge to brush his fingers across her cheek. But he didn't want to get scolded by the McQuaid men again. They were right to be looking out for her.

Before he could figure out what to say to her next, a distressed shout of his name came from the side road that led to the barn.

He scanned the area and located a woman near the parked conveyances of the guests. From the breathless rasp of her call, it was obvious she'd run to his house. And usually when that happened, the person was seeking him out for a medical emergency, either for herself or a family member.

Clearly hearing the urgency in the woman's tone, Astrid broke from him and began to stalk across the yard in the direction of the woman who was but an outline in the darkness. "I'm a doctor," Astrid called. "What is your need?"

The woman hesitated. "I need Dr. Steele."

"You can tell Dr. Nilsson," he replied. Astrid was every bit as competent as he was, and he wanted the people to see it.

"It's my husband." The woman's voice rang with despair. "He's fallen sick, and now one of my children is sick too."

Astrid hadn't lessened her stride, and Logan wound around the guests right behind her. "What are their symptoms?"

"They're complaining of headache, bones hurting, and feverishness. It happened so fast. They were fine at supper and now both are abed."

"Any rashes?" Astrid asked.

"Yes, the little one has a rash on his face. But it's my husband I'm most worried about. He's having a hard time."

Astrid stopped abruptly at the edge of the yard.

Logan almost bumped into her but found his footing just as she turned.

"Sounds like the influenza." In the light of a nearby lantern hanging from a post, her expression was grave.

"Yes, I would agree."

She swept her attention over the remaining guests, some sitting by the bonfire but most in the dance area awaiting the next round of music. "If it's the influenza, I'd like to diagnose it sooner rather than later. Do you mind if I take my leave from the party and make the house call?"

"Only if we can do it together."

Her eyes seemed to shine her approval. She gave a nod.

"Good. Then I'll get my bag, and we'll go."

13

"Is it the grippe?"

Astrid could hear the terror in the question passing through the upstairs room at the inn, where several families crowded together in a space that was meant for only one or two people. In the sparsely furnished room, bags were strewn about, and dirty clothing sat in heaps along with tattered blankets.

From what Astrid had gathered, the sick husband, his wife, and three children along with extended family had come looking for land, hoping to build cabins and get settled before winter came. They'd reached Fairplay and were tarrying at the inn while seeking employment and searching for the best place to live.

"Yes, it's the grippe." Astrid nodded the confirmation. Grippe. Influenza. It didn't matter what the people called it, the sickness was deadly. And it could spread faster than a wildfire on a windy mountain range.

She pressed a finger to the man's pulse, counting his heartbeats even as he thrashed in the throes of fever on the room's only bed.

His wife, her face haggard, perched on the opposite edge of the bed and was running a hand up and down her husband's shirtsleeve, clearly attempting to calm him.

Logan had his stethoscope positioned on the man's lungs and was listening for signs of fluid. There hadn't been any mention of coughing, so she was fairly certain the man didn't have consumption.

From what Astrid had witnessed of the influenza epidemic a couple of years ago, the best thing to do was air out the room of the bad vapors and work at keeping the bad blood from accumulating. "I'll stay with them but will need my satchel. I have quinine that might help."

Logan lifted his stethoscope, his brows furrowing above his impossibly dark eyes. "I'll stay with them. You go home." He nodded toward Charity Courtney waiting just outside the doorway. She'd asked to come with them and hoped to be of some help, explaining that she and her sisters had already had the influenza and survived it. "Can you drive Astrid back to the boardinghouse?"

The young woman stepped into the room. She raised her brows at Astrid as though to ask if she was agreeable to Logan's plan.

"I'm not going back, Logan." Astrid rose and grabbed a towel from the rack beside a basin. "I'm accustomed to facing all manner of illness and won't shirk away from anything now."

"I've already explained my position on germ theory." Logan moved from the bed and knelt beside a lad lying on a blanket on the floor. His eyes were open and glassy, a rash on his cheeks.

Unlike the majority of doctors who espoused the miasmal theory that infections were caused by poisonous airborne vapors, Logan argued for the less popular bacteriology model that claimed micro-organisms called germs transferred deadly substances among patients.

"Your astute theories have begun to sway my thinking in that direction." Quickly testing the water and finding it cold, she soaked the towel. "But in the case of influenza, everyone knows the miasma causes the spread."

"I disagree." Logan listened to the lad's lungs and heartbeat a moment longer before sitting up. "I believe the germs are causing the illness. I'm intending to set up a hospital of sorts for confining the sick and keeping them from passing it to more people. And since you haven't had influenza before, I'd like you to stay away, since I believe you would be more likely to catch the germs."

One of the older men sitting nearby shook his head and muttered, "Catchin' germs. What'll they think of next?"

Astrid lifted her chin and pulled herself up to her full height. "I took the Hippocratic Oath just as you did. And

I will not shirk my duty to the sick, even at great personal cost to myself."

He stood too, his expression growing stormy. "This is different—"

"This is no different than the dozens of people I've treated with the very same symptoms."

They locked eyes, his filling with concern. She appreciated his desire to keep her safe. But she needed him to understand that he couldn't shelter her from the worst or the most dangerous of cases just because she was a woman. If he truly believed she was an equal, then he had to treat her as an equal in all situations—including the influenza.

Charity cleared her throat loudly, drawing their attention. "If it's a hospital you're needing, we can set up one at my boardinghouse. It's out of the way, so it will be isolated. And my sisters and I can care for patients in the bedrooms as well as the living quarters. Pray to God we won't have need, but I can even make beds in the barn."

Logan gave a curt nod. "Good. I'll go with you."

"And so will I." Astrid focused on wringing the cool water from the towel.

Logan remained silent and stiff, but Charity started back through the doorway into the hall. "I'll go get my wagon, and we can begin transporting anyone with symptoms."

Astrid placed the cold cloth on the thrashing man's

forehead. Some physicians still believed in sweating the fever out of patients. Those same physicians often used bloodletting, blistering, and purging to return balance to the body's blood. But Astrid had studied the flaws in the theory of the four humors and had given up such treatments.

If she could adjust to the changing philosophies regarding fevers and humors, surely she could appreciate Logan's fine mind and his espousal of the germ theory.

She reached for another hand towel and dipped it in the cold water. "I'll submit to your ideas regarding germ theory in treating those with influenza if you'll agree to regard me with the same respect you would any male physician."

Logan tucked his stethoscope back into his bag. "I can regard you respectfully but still try to protect you from the influenza."

She wrung out the water, then placed the cool rag on the child's forehead. When she stood, she squared off with Logan. He'd crossed his arms, pulling his coat taut across his arms and shoulders, highlighting his strength. He'd taken off his hat, but otherwise looked as impeccable and gentlemanly as he had at the dance. And every bit as appealing.

As his dark eyes scanned down the length of her, likely taking note of her fancy gown and all her finery, her stomach began its all-too-common reaction to him, fluttering with warm desire. The touch of his lips on her neck during those last moments of dancing together still lingered. The brush of the kiss had been so unexpected, so stirring, that her knees had nearly given way.

And of course, it had only served to remind her of the way he'd kissed her for their official engagement kiss. All throughout the evening, every time she'd looked at Logan, she'd been tempted to study his mouth again, wanted to test it, needed to feel it against hers.

Now, the same need rushed back.

Quickly, before he realized the direction of her thoughts, she dropped her attention to the man in the bed and removed the towel from his forehead. It was already hot. She immersed it back in the water basin. "If I were a man, would you be convincing me not to do my job?"

Logan didn't respond.

She squeezed out the excess water and laid the towel across the man again. When finished, she glanced up. "W-e-l-l?"

"No." He spoke the word simply.

"That's my point—"

He took two large steps and stood in front of her. "You're not a man, though. You're my fiancée." His voice came out a low, hoarse whisper.

"No, I'm not," she hissed.

"Yes, you are."

Was he really serious about changing the nature of their relationship and making it real?

She wasn't sure what she'd been thinking when she'd brought up the possibility of going through with the wedding—had been wrapped up in the moment. Because the truth was, a relationship between them would be too complicated right now. She wasn't in a place in her life where she could leave Colorado—not until she made sure her consumption was well under control. And she had no idea how long that would take. Months. Possibly years. Maybe never.

She couldn't make him put his dreams and aspirations aside for her. She'd realized it that night at her sister's house when she'd started letting herself fall in love with him again.

Yes, she was falling in love with Logan Steele. How was it possible she was doing this a second time? Hadn't she learned anything from her previous heartache?

She kept her focus on his tie and kept her response a whisper. "I'm just your partner, Logan. I can't be anything more." No matter how much she might want to be with him, she couldn't hold on to him too tightly.

He stood unmoving for long seconds, his frustration palpable.

She didn't move either. She was staying strong in her resolve. She had to. For his sake so that she could set him free. A moment later, he spun, and his footsteps echoed loudly on the creaking floorboards.

Without a glance back, he exited the room and started down the stairs.

Astrid rode to the boardinghouse in the back of Charity's wagon with the two sick patients. Logan followed behind on his horse. When they arrived, they worked together to carry the patients up to one of the guest rooms. Astrid could sense Logan's hurt. But she decided some distance between them would only help them both regain much-needed perspective on the direction of their relationship.

Patience and Felicity rushed to help prepare beds and brought in cool water for attempting to control the fevers. Once the patients were settled, Astrid measured out enough quinine in tea for each of them and coaxed them to take sips.

Before leaving, Logan again tried to dissuade her from being involved. But she insisted that he shouldn't hold her to a different standard than he would a man.

Over the next few days, the influenza spread, just as they'd predicted. Logan kept office hours and continued his house calls, directing all people with symptoms to isolate at the Courtney Boardinghouse, close to town yet far enough away that they hoped they could contain the illness.

Meanwhile, Astrid remained busy at the makeshift hospital, cooling fevers, spooning liquids, measuring doses of quinine, and keeping the rooms aired.

After two days, the influenza had spread through the poorer area of Fairplay so that the sick and dying filled the upstairs, including Astrid's room. By the third day, the living quarters on the first floor were also lined with the sick, so that Astrid could hardly keep up with all the patients. She was grateful for the Courtney sisters' willingness to upend their lives and give over their home to care for the sick. They labored tirelessly alongside her day and night. And Logan came to help every spare moment he could when he wasn't tending to the sick in town.

As was to be expected, they couldn't save everyone. The father from the first sick family died, as did others. But Astrid was determined to save as many as possible. She slept for a few hours at a time here and there, ate infrequently, and changed clothing only because one of the children vomited on her.

By the fifth day, she was relieved to hear that no more new cases had developed. She wasn't sure if isolating the patients had stopped the spread or if a day of heavy rain had washed away the bad air. Whatever the case, she didn't rest and was determined to save her remaining patients.

During Logan's last visit to the house, she'd almost

told him that he'd worried about her for nothing. But she'd been too busy to do more than update him on the conditions of the patients who were faring the poorest.

It wasn't until after he'd left for the evening that she'd felt the first twinges of pain in her head and bones. Within a few hours, her temple pounded with an unending rhythm, and she could hardly move from her chair next to the bed of her youngest patient.

The lantern on the bedside table cast a soft glow over the boy's face. And though he was still feverish, the cool cloths seemed to be bringing his temperature down so that he was finally resting more peacefully.

The child's mother was lying in the bed beside him and was recuperating as well.

Astrid plunged the extra cloth into the basin of cool water on the bedside table, and instead of using it on the child, she pressed it against her cheek, the heat flowing off her now in waves.

She blinked back a surge of dizziness and shuffled the cloth to her forehead. She rested it there for a moment before releasing a tight breath. The moment she did, somehow a cough came out with it.

One little cough led to two. And before she knew it, her body was shuddering with coughs, and she was gasping with the effort of breathing. Though she couldn't feel the heaviness of fluid developing in her lungs, the wracking cough consumed her, until at last, she laid her head down on her arms on the edge of the bed.

The episode left her weak and even dizzier. She closed her eyes, her pulse beating much too fast and her airways constricting.

Forcing her head up, she put the towel back on her forehead. She had to face the truth. Not only did she have influenza, but her consumption was getting worse by the day. Several times over the past few days, she'd had to step outside during a coughing fit. She'd walked far enough into the woodland so that hopefully no one had heard her.

She twisted the engagement ring Logan had given her. It was gorgeous. She loved wearing it, admired it frequently, thought of him slipping it on each time she looked at it. But they had a fake engagement, and she would need to give him the ring back at some point.

Although she and Logan had been too consumed with the influenza to talk about anything else over the past few days, she'd caught him watching her a time or two as though he wanted to say more about their last conversation when she'd told him that they had to remain work partners and nothing more.

And this was why. Because ultimately she was a sick woman. She'd always been sick and ended up being a burden to the people around her. She couldn't do that to Logan.

"I'm sorry," she whispered. "I wish I were the right

woman for you, but I'm not."

She lifted the towel—now hot—from her face and attempted to place it in the basin. But her arm was too weak and bumped the container instead. Water sloshed over the edge, and the next thing she knew, the bowl was falling.

Her reflexes were too slow. Before she could grasp it, the basin clattered against the floor and shattered.

The child in the bed gave a startled cry, and the mother sat up, her eyes wild and filled with worry.

"Everything is alright." Astrid's words came out breathlessly. She bent to retrieve the broken pieces, but blackness weighed upon her. And in the next instant, she found herself toppling from the chair and plummeting to the floor, blessed unconsciousness claiming her.

14

Exhaustion weighed upon Logan, but in the low lantern light of his mother's spacious room, he helped her drink the last sip of the tea laced with morphine.

As she finished, her lashes fell against her pale cheeks, and she relaxed into her pillows, the medicine already taking the edge off the pain that was getting worse by the day. "Thank you, Logan," she whispered.

The large stove in the corner was burning, casting a warm glow over the room. A single oil lantern on the nearby pedestal table was also lit, its round floral-print globe turning the light to rose gold and highlighting the vases of freshly cut flowers he'd asked the servants to put around her room.

In the large bed with the intricately carved mahogany headboard and footboard, his mother was like a slight feather that had come loose from her pillow, easily lost among the covers.

The maidservant on night duty began to tuck the covers back around Mother's legs and arms. With rain having moved into the high country over the afternoon and evening, cooler temperatures had also arrived, a relief from the July heat for most people. But not for Mother. Even when the summer heat had been stifling, his mother had been constantly cold. The chilled air only made her more so.

He pressed his stethoscope against her chest, the soft thud of her heartbeat pulsing strongly. Then he squeezed her hand, the bones more prominent than they'd been even a week ago. She hadn't eaten well all week, and he guessed the increased pain was diminishing her appetite.

He hated that he'd been so busy and hadn't been able to spend as much time with her in the evenings as he usually did. But the outbreak of influenza had taken his every effort, especially in his attempts to convince those who had the symptoms to stay in their homes if they could. For those who couldn't isolate, he'd sent them to Courtney Boardinghouse.

He'd done his best to check on the patients at the boardinghouse, but he'd been so overwhelmed with the needs of those who were sick in town and in the outlying areas that he hadn't been able to keep up with everything.

What would he have done without Astrid's help?

He rubbed a hand over his eyes. He'd been unfair to her at the outset of the influenza, the night of the dance.

She'd asked him to let her do her job just as any man would have done. But the truth was that he'd been scared he'd lose her to the illness before he really had the chance to be with her. Because, whether he was ready to admit it or not, he cared about Astrid more than he'd ever cared about any other woman.

He wasn't sure how his feelings for her had gained leverage so quickly. Maybe they'd lain dormant inside him from their past. Maybe she was simply the woman he'd been waiting for, the one who could make him forget about all his hesitations regarding marriage and family. Or maybe all the prodding by his mother had moved their relationship along more rapidly than normal.

Whatever the case, he couldn't deny that his feelings for Astrid were strong—so strong that he'd been unable to truly draw in a breath at the end of every day until he'd gone out to the boardinghouse and seen for himself that she was okay.

"Logan?" His mother's whisper was faint.

"I'm here." Tenderly, he stroked her hand. "Go back to sleep."

"I don't think I'll make it to the wedding."

A fresh knot of guilt tangled in his gut—guilt he'd been trying to ignore all week whenever she'd regaled him with the wedding details that she was busy arranging. From what the maids and other servants had told him, she'd spent every waking moment on wedding plans.

They'd informed him that it was the one thing that kept her busy and her mind off her pain.

A part of him warned that he had to put a stop to her planning and make up some kind of excuse for why he and Astrid couldn't get married after the three weeks.

But another part of him went back to Astrid's shy comment at the dance when she'd asked if they should go through with it. She wouldn't have brought up the possibility if she truly viewed him as her partner and nothing more. She did feel something for him. But was it enough for her to give up her life here in Colorado and go east with him?

And was he ready to make such a big change to his life by taking a wife? After years of resisting, could he switch his plans?

The alternative—leaving her behind and living without her—was growing more difficult to fathom.

Next time he saw her, he'd ask her to take a walk, or at least find a private spot where they could have a conversation about how to handle the impending nuptials. In the meantime, he'd simply have to continue telling his mother what she needed to hear—anything to make her happy during these last days of her life.

"Don't worry, Mother. If you can't make it downstairs to the parlor, we can have the wedding right here in your bedroom."

"No. Not *make it* like that. I mean *make it* as in the

number of days."

He wanted to contradict her. But all along he'd been honest with her regarding her prognosis. He didn't want to start lying about that too.

"That's why I suggest we move the wedding to next Saturday morning."

Inwardly, he groaned. "That's only eight days from now."

"Yes, I'm aware of that."

"With the uncertainty of the influenza—"

"We'll keep it small." Her voice was growing slurred.

"It's too soon."

She opened her eyes, and tears welled up. "I don't want to miss it."

Deuces. How could he promise his mother a wedding next Saturday when Astrid hadn't agreed to marry him at all?

He pressed his fingers against his tired eyes, as if that could somehow block out the problem. Could he convince Astrid? With her admission that she wanted marriage and a family, maybe he'd be able to talk her into it.

But that wasn't what he wanted. To coerce a woman into marrying him so that he didn't have to disappoint his dying mother. He couldn't do that to Astrid. He could only take this charade so far.

"Mother." He had to admit to his crazy scheme.

Honesty was the only way forward. In fact, if he'd been honest from the start, he could have avoided the whole predicament altogether. "I have to tell you something—"

"No, don't say anything more tonight." She closed her eyes and exhaled a rattling breath. "Just think about it, alright?"

"Alright." He could promise her that.

At a pounding against the front door below, he sighed. It was likely someone coming to ask him to help with another influenza case, probably one of the many who'd taken a turn for the worse.

If only he had a better way to fight his mother's illness. Even after arriving in Fairplay, he'd done his best to keep abreast of recent medical news and procedures, devouring each journal that arrived in the mail—the *Lancet*, the *New England Journal of Medicine*, and others. But unfortunately, none had offered any hope of curing cancer.

He pulled out his pocket watch and held it by the lantern. Half past midnight. He'd only been home for an hour, had been looking forward to dropping into his bed and falling into a dreamless and heavy sleep where he didn't have to worry about anything.

Stuffing the watch back, he bent and placed a kiss on his mother's forehead, her skin as flaky as dry paper.

She didn't respond, her heavy, steady breathing telling him that she'd fallen asleep—hopefully devoid of pain, at least for a few hours.

He rounded the bed and tossed his usual instructions to the maidservant who was adding fuel to the stove in the corner. "Try to get her to drink warm broth, and keep giving her calomel. If she starts to grow uncomfortable, administer a dose of brandy with the arrowroot laudanum."

He didn't wait for an acknowledgement but hurried from the room and down the hallway. As he descended the stairs, the butler stood at the open front door in his housecoat, nightcap, and slippers. The lantern he held illuminated a woman on the front porch, shrouded in a man's greatcoat and battered hat, both slick with rain.

At the sight of a red braid, his pulse picked up pace. "Miss Courtney?"

She tipped up the brim of the too-big hat, giving him a glimpse of the worry in her wide eyes.

"Dr. Steele." Her voice held a note that was dissonant, like an off-key piano chord.

He hurried his last steps to the door. "What is it?"

"I thought you'd want to know. Astrid—Dr. Nilsson—has fallen ill with influenza."

His heart had already ceased beating, leaving only a hollow ache in his chest cavity. "When?" He managed to push the one word out.

"She collapsed just a little bit ago. My sisters are watching her—"

"How bad?" His question came out harsh. But he was tumbling into the sinking emptiness inside him and was trying to brace himself for the impact.

"She's burning up badly. I believe she's probably had it a while and didn't say anything."

The despair rose up to slam hard against him. His knees, his legs, his body felt suddenly weak. He grabbed on to the door frame, and in the next instant, the butler was at his side, bracing him up.

"I came right away." Charity's shoulders slumped as though feeling the despair as much as he was. She'd been a saint to turn her home into a makeshift hospital, housing, feeding, and caring for the sick without a word of complaint. Surely, watching some of the ill die had brought back painful memories of losing her parents, and he couldn't selfishly focus on himself and his own frustrations.

"Thank you, Miss Courtney." He squeezed the words past his tight throat. "I'll saddle up and ride out right away."

At the patter of footsteps down the hallway, he guessed one of the servants was already heading to the barn to inform the groomsman to ready his mount. As he straightened and reached for the nearest coat on the towering coat tree, he willed himself to remain strong.

Charity turned to go, but then stopped. "You should know, Astrid is suffering from another illness too."

He fumbled with his coat, but it slipped through his fingers and fell to the floor. "How so?" Even before she spoke the words, he knew what she was going to say.

"Consumption." He whispered the word at the same time Charity did.

His mind replayed his interactions with Astrid. Over the past two weeks she'd been back in Fairplay, he hadn't noticed trouble breathing, fever, coughing, or pale skin.

But that didn't mean she wasn't experiencing a resurgence of the dreaded White Death. Since she'd once had consumption, it was possible that she'd never recovered fully, that the consumption had merely been checked enough that she could resume normal life. It had likely lain dormant and was now beginning to express itself again.

"What are the prevailing symptoms?" he asked.

Charity hung her head, the hat slipping back down and shadowing her face. "I hear her coughing at night when she thinks everyone is asleep. And this week, it's gotten so bad that she goes outside to cough where she doesn't think anyone can hear her."

The rumble of thunder resounded in the foothills, the signal of another storm rolling in. And a gust of cold air pushed inside the open door and slapped at Logan, waking him up, driving out the exhaustion he'd felt only a short while ago.

If Astrid was already fighting against consumption,

how would she have the strength to also battle influenza?

He drew in a shaky breath, praying for vitality and strength for his own body. He was going to need every ounce he could gather, because he intended to wage war for her as he had for no one else ever before.

Logan laid a hand against Astrid's forehead. Her skin was burning up.

He skimmed his fingers down her cheek to her neck and paused to time her pulse. As he silently counted, he surveyed the rest of her body—limp and weak and motionless. Atop her bed and still attired in the clothing she'd worn for the past couple of days, she was disheveled, her bodice stained with bodily fluids, a dirty apron tied haphazardly over her skirt, and her hair askew from her normal tidy chignon.

For as impeccably as she always presented herself, her state of unkemptness was a sign of just how busy she'd been and how little she'd taken care of herself. Even though he'd told her she needed to rest earlier, before he'd taken his leave, he should have insisted she go to bed.

The lack of sleep along with the stress had likely contributed to the worsening of the consumption. And in a weakened state, she would have been more susceptible to the influenza germs.

His heart thundered in rhythm with the booming of the storm that had moved in during his ride to the boardinghouse. He was dripping wet and his hair plastered to his forehead. But he didn't care. All that mattered was finding a way to bring Astrid's fever down.

"Draw Astrid a bath." He shot the words over his shoulder to one of the Courtney sisters. "Tepid water—not warm, but not cold enough to shock her system."

Thankfully, the sisters had already moved everyone out of Astrid's room and had cleaned it and changed the sheets on her bed. He supposed it wasn't fair that the other patients would have to crowd together in the remaining rooms, but he wanted to keep Astrid apart from the others so that he could tend to her without interruption.

He dug in his satchel for his stethoscope. As he pressed it against her chest, he quietened his thoughts and pulse, both of which had been racing since Charity had brought him the news about Astrid falling sick.

He let himself take in her face again—her delicate features, her long lashes, her flushed cheeks, and her perfectly rounded lips. Even when she was sick, she was still the most beautiful woman on earth and in heaven.

How could he bear losing her? Not so soon after reuniting with her. Not after having such a short time together. Not after his mother passed away. Not ever.

There it was. The truth. He didn't want to lose her.

Rain drummed against the rooftop overhead, and wind rattled the windowpane as if to protest the revelation. But it was a weak effort. He could no longer deny that he was more than ready to marry her, that his desire for her outweighed his fear of becoming like his father.

Maybe his mother had seen what he'd tried to ignore—that he wasn't meant for singleness, that he would be richer and fuller and more complete with a woman by his side. Maybe he'd just needed the right woman to come along and show him that. And Astrid was the right woman, quite possibly the only woman for him.

Was he already falling in love with her?

He straightened and nearly bumped his head on the slanted ceiling. She'd always been very special to him, special enough that even when he'd returned east, he'd thought of her, more so during those early years.

She shifted her head back and forth and released a soft moan. She was likely feeling the full effects of the influenza—aching joints, a pounding headache, along with dizziness and delirium.

He stuffed the stethoscope back into his bag and then dug around, pulling out several bottles—calomel, quinine, and arsenic. Although the arsenic was a poisonous agent, the tincture, in a miniscule dosage, could help reduce her fever.

"I need a cup of hot water." He shot another order over his shoulder only to find Charity waiting behind him, her clothes as dripping wet as his.

"How is she?" The young woman's pretty face was lined with worry and weariness. How long had it been since Charity and her sisters had slept? Maybe he ought to move everyone from the boardinghouse back into town.

Even as he considered such an option, he quickly thrust it aside. With the outbreak mostly contained, he didn't want to chance anyone else catching it.

"We need to bring down her fever." He swished the bottle of arsenic. "I'll give her some medicine. Then I'll sponge her down in a bath of cool water."

"I'll give her the bath."

"Not necessary. I intend to take care of her."

Charity lowered her head, color infusing her face. "Doctor, I know Astrid would be embarrassed once she awakened to learn you had undressed her and given her a bath."

His thoughts came to an abrupt halt at the image of working the buttons of her bodice free. Even if he'd had his fair share of encounters with the human body— including female bodies—over the years, he'd always viewed each person objectively and clinically.

But with Astrid? Even though he'd never in a million years consider taking advantage of her, sick or otherwise, he knew Charity was right. Astrid would be mortified if he took care of her personal needs.

He didn't need to argue with Charity any further. He merely nodded. Tonight wasn't his night for the undressing and bathing. Tonight he was fighting for her life.

If he fought hard enough, then maybe someday he'd be able to hold her again, dance with her in the moonlight, and kiss the thudding pulse in her neck. Then after pulling her close and whispering in her ear how much he adored her, he'd relish popping open each button and kissing each inch of bare skin underneath.

Astrid thrashed for most of the night, her fever escalating with every passing hour no matter what course of treatment he prescribed and no matter what medicines he administered. He stepped out of her room several times to allow Charity the chance to soak Astrid in the bathtub of cool water that one of the sisters had dutifully brought to the room and filled.

The baths seemed to help for a short duration, but the fever always came raging back.

He laboriously spooned broth, tea, water, and tinctures into her mouth. And he spent hours laying cool cloths over her forehead, along with wiping down her cheeks, neck, and arms. The cotton chemise Charity had put on Astrid was light and allowed for the ever-cooling air of the night to soothe her heated skin too.

But by morning, in spite of his constant attention, she was growing weaker and more lethargic. He'd only slept five minutes here and there throughout the night and suspected Charity hadn't rested much more than he had.

She entered the room as the first light of dawn began to chase away the long shadows of the night, and passed him a steaming mug of coffee. She didn't say anything to him about needing to leave Astrid's side or sleep or take care of other patients. He was grateful for that. Because he wouldn't have left, not even if she'd pleaded with him.

He asked her to send word to his mother of Astrid's illness along with instructions for the servants regarding administering more pain medicine. He also advised Charity to send word to Greta.

He loathed that he had to apprise Astrid's sister of the gravity of her illness. But he didn't want to neglect letting her know. If Astrid didn't make it through the day, Greta deserved to say goodbye.

By mid-afternoon, the entire McQuaid family waited outside the boardinghouse. Logan made sure they didn't come too close, and the only one he allowed in was Greta, much to the dismay of everyone else.

Greta sat in the chair beside the bed, held Astrid's hand, and let silent tears fall unchecked.

Logan waited just outside the doorway, giving Greta privacy. He wanted to be the one beside Astrid during her final moments, but he couldn't deny that privilege to Greta, even though his heart was being ripped to shreds with the need to be with Astrid.

"You should be here too, Logan." Greta finally peered over her shoulder at him and held out her hand, beckoning him into the room.

Logan shoved away from the wall where he'd been leaning and ducked back into the room. The sunshine washed the room with a cheerful glow, as if it were laughing in their faces and ignoring how serious the occasion was.

He'd already closed the curtains in a rebellious effort to defy the sunshine. And now, he wanted to rant about how he couldn't give up, how he'd keep fighting for her. Instead, he approached the bed and stood beside Greta.

Greta lifted Astrid's hand and pressed a kiss to it. "Did Astrid ever tell you that your father was the one who arranged my marriage to my husband on the night I arrived in Fairplay?"

"She mentioned it long ago."

Greta's lips lifted into a wistful smile. "Your father was anxious to create a civil town with lots of families and children so that you and your mother would be willing to live here."

Logan shook his head. "No, my father wasn't

interested in my mother or me. He saw us as a nuisance."

"Oh my, no." Greta's smile lifted. "Your father could hardly talk of anything but you and your mother. In fact, he was so eager to grow the town that he wanted us to start having children right away so that you'd have friends here."

"Are we speaking of the same man?" Logan released a soft scoffing laugh. "The day my father walked out of the house and left for the West, he told my mother he needed his freedom."

Greta's pretty brow furrowed. "Your father built the house, school, and a dozen other businesses all with the purpose of making the town attractive to you and your mother."

"I don't think so."

"I know so." Her voice turned firm. "If not for your father's desire to be with you and your mother, I wouldn't have married Wyatt, and Astrid and I might never have remained in Fairplay."

His father had never acted as though he desired to be with him and Mother. Mother had always said she'd been the one to finally suggest that the two of them move to Colorado.

Greta pressed another kiss to Astrid's hand. "You should be grateful to your father. If not for him, you never would have met Astrid."

Grateful to his father? Greta clearly had his father

mixed up with someone else. Or perhaps his father had said one thing to the people of Fairplay to make himself look like a family man, when in reality, he'd all but abandoned his wife and son.

"And then you wouldn't have fallen for her," Greta added softly, peering up at him with the same silver-blue eyes as Astrid. The sight of the exquisite color tore at Logan's heart. And her words tore at him as well.

Yes, he had fallen for her. That was inarguable.

"I don't know exactly what motivated you and Astrid to move so quickly into a relationship and engagement. I suspect I don't want to know." Greta's voice was gentle, but it contained a firmness as well. Was she telling him that she knew Astrid wouldn't have rushed into any of it unless he'd pressured her in some way?

If so, she was right.

Should he admit to the truth about coercing her into a courtship for his mother's sake? Now that Astrid was dying, what difference did it make who knew?

"Whatever the reason was for your haste," Greta continued before he could say anything, "I can tell you love her, Logan. Really love her. And in the end, that's really all that matters."

The pain in his chest swelled swiftly, stinging the backs of his eyes.

Heaven, have mercy. Greta was right. He did love Astrid. He loved everything about her—her determined spirit, intelligence, compassion, and of course, her beautiful body. The truth was, he'd probably been in love with her when he'd left for Boston, and he'd probably fallen in love again the day she'd shown up in his office and slapped him across the face. There was no reason not to admit it—not anymore, now that she was . . .

His gaze landed upon her flushed face. What he wouldn't give at this moment to have her open her eyes and peer up at him with all her feistiness.

"Yes, I love her." His confession came out strangled. "And I don't want to lose her."

Panic rose into his throat to choke him. He couldn't just stand by and let her die. He wanted—no, needed—more time with her. In fact, he wanted a lifetime with her, but he'd take any amount he could get.

"Charity?" He called through the open doorway. "Bring more cool water. We're giving Astrid another bath."

At the rapid footsteps hurrying to do his bidding, he opened his doctor satchel and dug through it as he had already a dozen times, searching for anything else he could give her.

Steely determination crept up his backbone. He wouldn't rest. He wasn't done fighting. And he wouldn't be as long as Astrid still had breath.

16

Astrid felt as though she were burning alive. The heat of flames licked her skin and roasted her flesh like medieval torture.

At one point, she roused to find Greta sitting in the chair beside the bed. Sometimes Logan's face hovered near. Other times she awoke to cool water covering her in a bath. But all the while, the fire continued to sear her. Until at last, blessedly, the pain ceased.

She had the strange feeling that perhaps she'd died and that her soul had separated from her body. But the next time she woke, she realized that someone was holding her hand and singing softly. Someone sounding like Greta.

She pried open her eyes to find that Greta really was there, in a chair next to her bed, daylight spilling around her.

"Greta?"

Greta jolted forward, her beautiful face hovering above Astrid's—almost a mirror image, but more solid and sturdy and healthy in a way that Astrid had never been and might never be. "Yes, it's me."

"I'm thirsty."

Greta smoothed a hand over Astrid's forehead and then cheek before calling over her shoulder. "I think her fever has broken."

"The influenza?" Astrid managed, her throat dry and tight.

With tears sliding down her cheeks, Greta smiled. "You're going to make it."

"How long have I been sick?"

"Two days."

Astrid tried to take stock of where she was—the small room, the slanted ceiling, the lacy curtains in the window, the simply decorated room with handstitched quilts and lovely watercolor paintings. She was still in Fairplay at the Courtney Boardinghouse.

And Logan? Where was he?

She strained to see past Greta.

Greta swiped at the tears flowing down her cheeks and smiled. "Logan's on his way up. I hear his footsteps on the stairs."

An instant later, Logan charged into the room, his presence as powerful and commanding as always. He flew to the bed and towered above her, his dark hair tousled and his facial scruff thick. His white shirt was unbuttoned at the collar, and he was without his usual vest and coat. But he'd never looked more appealing. She wanted to drag him down and hold him and never let him go.

His gaze raked over her before coming to rest upon her face. His brows were furrowed and his face etched with weariness. But his eyes were filled with hope. And overwhelming relief.

He dropped to the side of the bed and laid a hand on her forehead. "How are you feeling?"

"Tired."

He brushed his fingers across her temple, then down to her cheeks.

Closing her eyes, she leaned into his hand. His touch was so tender.

But his hand lifted from her all too soon. And before she could tell him she wanted him to go on caressing her forever, she drifted into a peaceful sleep.

The next time she awoke, the bright sunshine had vanished, and dark shadows had fallen.

At a soft shuffling noise coming from beside the bed, Astrid shifted her head on the pillow. "Greta?"

The person wasn't Greta. Instead, the woman in the bedside chair startled, sat forward, and stopped brushing what appeared to be glue of some kind over a glass vase that was covered in colorful paper. With lovely features and long blond hair twisted into a simple bun, the woman gave Astrid a kind smile.

Astrid couldn't think past the fog in her brain. Where was Greta? Or Logan? And who was this woman? She studied the young face with the charcoal smudge and paint smear until the name registered. Patience. The middle Courtney sister.

Patience set aside her artistic creation and reached for a mug on the bedside table. "Let's see if we can get you to drink this broth. Dr. Steele insisted we get you to have more."

Astrid allowed the young woman to help her sit up against the pillows and took several small sips of the greasy water that had a chicken flavor.

"Is Logan here?" Astrid glanced past Patience to the door, waiting for Logan to come rushing in as he had the last time.

Patience held the mug near Astrid's mouth. "He went home to check on his mother and to make rounds among those who are still ill with the influenza."

"Oh." Astrid couldn't keep the disappointment from rising and clogging her throat. In fact, the need to be with him swelled so fiercely that her eyes pricked with tears. She was being selfish for wanting him so badly. He had other responsibilities besides her. And she didn't want to be the cause of him not being able to spend time with his mother during her last days.

Regardless, the need for him was powerful.

"And Greta?" She took another sip and swallowed.

"She left earlier today when your fever broke, once she knew that you were going to make it."

Astrid tried to remember everything that had happened, but the past few days were just fragmented pieces that didn't fit together. "So I was close to dying?"

"No one except for Logan believed you'd pull through. He didn't give up but kept using every trick he'd ever learned to keep you alive."

She'd have to ask him later what he'd done. But for now, she was relieved and grateful that she was still breathing. She'd watched too many others die earlier in the week and knew the same could have happened to her.

Astrid took another drink, but the liquid caught in her throat. She coughed to dislodge the tickle, but as soon as she did so, the motion irritated the lining of her bronchi, as it usually did. And before she knew it, she was having one of her coughing spells, one where she couldn't catch her breath.

The commotion brought both Charity and Felicity to the room, and within moments the three young sisters were fanning her and patting her back, all in an effort to stop the coughing. Finally, Astrid fell against her pillows, her airways tight, her respirations too fast.

"I'm sorry." Her words were raspy and followed by a wheeze.

"You're not to worry." Charity smoothed back Astrid's hair, reminding her of Greta. She could only imagine how worried Greta had been, sitting by her bedside—how it must have taken Greta back to the time when Astrid had been sick as a child.

Was this a premonition of what was to come? Would she inevitably end up back at Healing Springs Ranch, weak and in bed, with Greta having to nurse her again? She knew Greta would have it no other way.

A wave of weariness rolled through Astrid. If she were honest with herself, she could admit that was one of the reasons why she'd returned home. Because when the end came, she didn't want to be alone.

For now, though, she was still strong. She wouldn't let the consumption immobilize her and intended to keep going as long as she could.

She sat up and started to swing her legs over the edge of the bed. "How many patients are still here?"

Charity tsked and immediately lifted Astrid's legs back under the covers. "All but five have gone home."

Astrid tried to push the blankets away again. "I'd like to take a look at everyone, see how they're doing."

"No." Charity held her firmly in place. "Dr. Steele said not to let you out of bed. In fact, he gave us permission to tie you down if you didn't obey."

Yes, she really ought to stay abed and recuperate longer. Even so, she'd always had to fight to gain everything in her life, and she'd forgotten what it was like to rest. "Logan Steele likes to get his way."

"That may be, but I've never seen anyone work as hard as he did for you."

Astrid lay back, too weak to fight. "He's a good doctor." She'd met few physicians who equaled him in skill. It was no wonder Mass Medical College was seeking him out as a lecturer. Only the top doctors were offered such honors.

Charity brought the covers up to Astrid's chin. "His efforts to save your life went beyond him being just a *good doctor*." Charity began to move about the room, collecting bowls and mugs and basins. "That man is plain crazy about you. He would have done anything to save you, including giving you his own life if he could have."

"You're wrong." Astrid lowered her lashes halfway so that Charity couldn't see her embarrassment. Should she tell the young woman the truth about her and Logan and their fake engagement?

"I'm not wrong. I saw his desperation. He loves you—"

"Our engagement isn't real." The words tumbled out, the guilt too heavy to bear any longer.

Nearing the door, Charity paused, both hands full of dishes. Her brows rose, reflecting the surprise in her eyes.

Astrid pushed up to her elbows. Now that she'd started a confession, she might as well finish. "Logan persuaded me to start courting in order to make his mother happy. Our fake relationship was supposed to be simple—spending time together once in a while, sitting together at church, that sort of thing."

Charity's lips curved up into the beginning of a smile. "What the two of you feel for each other is anything but fake or simple."

"It's gotten out of control. His mother assumed we were engaged, and one thing led to another."

Charity's smile widened. "It looks like it led exactly where it needed to, giving you both the opportunity to let old feelings for each other blossom again."

The feelings had resurged with more than just a few blossoms. Her feelings had come back like a lush garden with all varieties of flowers in full bloom. She hadn't meant to let it happen, but somehow it had anyway.

"Seems to me," Charity continued, "you'll be healthy and back on your feet just in time for that wedding Mrs. Steele is busy planning."

Charity exited before Astrid could object any further. She knew she needed to say something, but for now, she simply sank back against the mattress and pillows, letting Charity's words sift through her: *That man is plain crazy about you. He loves you.*

Warmth spread through her insides, almost as if she'd

swallowed a hot infusion. As her eyelids grew heavy and sleep beckoned her, she wrapped her arms closer, wanting to relish, even if only for a few moments, the possibility that Logan truly did love her.

17

Logan awoke with a start.

The room was dark, the lantern extinguished. And someone had covered him with a blanket—probably Charity.

He hadn't wanted to leave Astrid's bedside earlier. But once her fever had broken and he'd known she would live, he'd had no more excuse for neglecting his mother or the other patients who needed his care.

He'd already told his mother of Astrid's illness during one of his brief stops home. She'd been praying fervently for Astrid's recovery, and when he'd brought her the news that Astrid would survive, she'd started weeping. After she'd dried her tears, she'd insisted that the wedding continue as planned, even if Astrid was still sick.

And this time, he hadn't offered one word of protest, not even the slightest.

All throughout the evening, he'd hardly stopped or

dared to breathe until he'd returned to the boardinghouse, rushed up the stairs, and glimpsed Astrid sleeping peacefully on her bed. Then he'd dropped into the chair beside her and hadn't moved since.

A cough broke the silence. Astrid's cough. Likely what had startled him awake in the first place.

He sat forward and skimmed a hand across the mattress until he made contact with her arm. With proficient fingers even in the dark, he found the pulse in her neck and counted her heartbeats. Before he could finish, she coughed again, this time more deeply.

Was it dry or wet? One that was developing as a result of her influenza? Or was this the consumption, the coughing that Charity had overheard on other occasions?

He groped for his satchel beside his chair and quickly located his stethoscope. Before he could situate it around his neck, Astrid's cough deepened, and she pushed up from the mattress, gasping for breath.

Bare footsteps slapped down the hallway toward the room, and a moment later Charity entered, a candle in hand. The light cast a glow over Astrid's face. She was pale and her eyes filled with distress because she couldn't draw in a full breath.

He stood and started toward the window. "We need to get her some fresh air."

"I'll make a tonic for her—with a family recipe."

"Thank you. Anything to soothe her throat." He

muscled against the window, the frame rasping and sticking with every push up he made. Somehow he managed to open it enough to allow a gust of night breeze inside. He'd heard that fresh air—especially cold—had a way of helping those with consumption.

But even as the cool air wove through the room, she continued to cough, unable to stop.

The same desperation he'd felt when she'd been sick with influenza reared up like a wild mountain lion ready to ambush its prey. He'd saved her once, and he wouldn't let anything stand in the way of saving her again.

With a growl, he bent, slipped his arms underneath her, and drew her up so that he was cradling her against his chest.

Her blankets fell away, but he didn't stop to gather them. Instead, he stalked toward the open window and let the breeze engulf them both. It was moist and cool, and he prayed it would bring her some relief.

"All you have to do is get some air." He tried to keep his voice calm and steady. From the stiffness of her body and limbs, he could sense that her anxiety was continuing to mount. And worry would only exacerbate the issue.

She lifted her face and her nose, trying to breathe in. She dragged in a wheezing gasp, but then hacked again.

"Little breaths," he urged, every nerve and muscle aching with the need to bring her relief. "Just little breaths, Astrid."

She nodded and tried to shorten her efforts.

"That's right." He brushed a kiss across her forehead, unable to stop himself. "Keep trying."

With the next respiration, the coughing seemed to diminish.

"There. You're going to be just fine." He prayed he was right, but with how rapidly her coughing had spiraled out of control and how violent it had become, he guessed it wouldn't be long before she was coughing up blood.

He had to find a way to help her before that happened. But how? Consumption had been raging through the United States and many other countries around the world for the past few decades. Numerous pathologists and other scientists had proposed various antidotes, but so far no one had been able to find a cure.

For long moments, he stood with her beside the open window, until at last, her coughing spluttered into wheezing. She was so still that he guessed she'd gone back to sleep, that the consumption was simply too much for her already weakened system to handle.

"Dr. Steele?" Charity's soft call came from behind him. "I have the tonic ready."

As he turned, the glow from the candlelight on the bedside table highlighted the flush on Astrid's cheeks from her exertion, the shallowness of each inhale, and the lethargic way she slumped against him, resting her head on his shoulder.

He nodded at Charity. "I'll keep holding her in front of the window while you see if you can get her to drink it."

Astrid didn't resist their efforts and dutifully sipped the tonic, which was made of apple cider vinegar, warm water, and honey. When finally she seemed to be resting against him more comfortably, he lowered himself into the chair that Charity had positioned in front of the open window so that the breeze bathed Astrid's face.

Once more Astrid was asleep, her cheek pressed against his shoulder.

"Are you sure you don't want me to stay with her?" Charity hesitated in the doorway, candle in hand.

"I can't leave her." Worry was woven through his whisper with strings that were wrapped around his heart and tugging hard.

Charity lingered another moment, then spoke again, her voice tinged with embarrassment. "Now that she's mending, perhaps I should be the one to remain by her side through the night . . ."

He understood what she was implying. But he wasn't leaving her. "She's too sick, and I'm too tired. Nothing indecent will happen."

Charity ducked her head as if the mere mention of the word *indecent* was itself indecent. "If you need anything, just call." Then she scurried away.

He situated Astrid more comfortably. With the

blankets surrounding her, she was covered except for her face and her hair. Gently, he combed his fingers through the long silky strands that had come loose from her braid. Then he traced a tender path around her face.

The faint moonlight coming in the window provided him enough light that he could see her delicate features, her long lashes, and her lips—the slightly upturned and extremely kissable lips.

Yes, he intended to kiss her good and hard and long. Just not tonight. Not until he was certain she was completely on the mend.

After almost losing her, one thing had become abundantly clear. He didn't want to be apart from her ever again.

The fact was, even without his mother's rushing, he wanted to move things along. If her consumption was returning, then he might not have a great deal of time left with her. And he didn't want to waste a single second.

Now, he just had to figure out a way to convince her to agree to marry him in less than a week, on Saturday as his mother wanted.

But how? What could he do?

At some point, he dozed. When he awoke, Astrid was shivering, the blankets having come untucked. The night air had grown too cold, and yet he didn't want to eliminate the fresh air.

Rather than close the window, he opted for moving her out of the breeze. He carried her back to her bed, and as he lowered her, she tightened her arms around his neck.

"I'm so cold," she mumbled even as she shuddered.

He tried to tuck the covers back around her, but even then, she didn't let go.

"Warm me up, Logan." Her murmur was sleepy.

He hesitated at the side of the bed, still bent over her. He glanced at the empty spot on the mattress beside her, then at the open door. What harm could come from resting beside her for a few minutes? He'd make sure she was bundled securely in the blankets, and only then would he wrap his arms around her and lend her his warmth.

"Please?" she asked, finally opening her eyes halfway. "Keep holding me."

She probably meant for him to rest with her in the chair again, but now that they were here at the bed, what difference would it make if he held her in the chair or on the bed?

Gently, he lowered himself to his side next to her. He tried to keep some distance between them, but the sagging mattress seemed determined to press them together, and he found his body flush against hers.

She situated her head on his shoulder and her face in the crook of his neck. And within seconds she was breathing steadily again, the sign she'd fallen back asleep.

What would it be like to pull her into his arms every night? Just like this.

He closed his eyes and breathed her in. Somehow with her, and only with her, his life was more complete and his burdens not so weighty.

Ever since returning to Colorado, his heart had been heavy. Yes, his mother's impending death was difficult. But after the past eight years of physician training and practice, death was no longer a stranger to him, and he'd watched enough people die to know that he couldn't stop the grave from claiming who it would.

If he was really honest, the heaviness inside had more to do with his father and their strained relationship. Maybe he'd held on to the hope that someday his father would feel sorrow over abandoning him and Mother. But maybe such a confession was too much to hope for. Maybe he had to finally accept that his father would never own up to his mistakes.

Could he live with that? And maybe even put his past behind him?

Whatever the case, since having Astrid back in his life, he'd felt as though he wasn't alone anymore and had strength to face his difficulties. It was the same way he'd felt when she'd offered him friendship after he'd first moved to Fairplay. It was almost as if she was the sunshine that broke through the storms in his life. How had he gotten along without her?

He allowed himself to sink back, then closed his eyes and situated his chin on her head. He'd rest beside her for an hour or two to warm her up. Then he'd get up and sit in the chair. That's all. Nothing more.

18

Astrid stretched only to find arms tightening around her. Strong manly arms. A long lean body. The earthy-spicy scent of cologne.

She was still with Logan. Right where she wanted to be.

As she opened her eyes, she could sense that she was recovered from the influenza. The fever was gone, her bones no longer ached, and the exhaustion wasn't weighing upon her. Even her coughing spells seemed part of a bad dream.

The faint light breaking through the darkness told her dawn was almost upon them, and it wouldn't be long before the Courtney sisters rose and started their morning chores. She ought to get up, too, and lend them a hand now that she was better. But the chill of the night hung heavily in the room, and she snuggled deeper under her covers.

At her movement, Logan's fingers grazed her back, as if he was soothing her even in his sleep. And from the steady rise and fall of his chest and his even breathing, she could tell he was getting much-needed slumber.

Her hand rested against his heart, and she could feel the steady beat of his pulse. And she could feel that his shirt was unbuttoned halfway. The casualness was like an invitation to let her mind take a walk down the rest of him. His cotton undershirt stretched taut over his chest, his suspenders hung loose at his waist, and his trousers rode low on his hips.

Logan Steele was a fine, fine man, and here she was beside him and in his arms. Her insides began to turn slushy, melting like snow and ice after a long winter. The thawing puddles were oozing, and she wanted nothing more than to sink into the sensation, sink into him, sink into whatever this was she was feeling for him.

His leg shifted against hers. His leg that was tangled with hers.

Heaven, have mercy. Was that his knee wedged between hers? And was her nightgown really bunched up at her thighs?

Oh dear. Oh dear. Oh dear. What had happened? What were they doing?

Panic burst through her, turning all the warm liquids back into solids. No more melting, thawing, and sinking. She had to get back on firm ground, which meant extricating herself before another influenza patient or one of the Courtney sisters happened into the room and caught them in bed together this way.

Drawing in a steadying breath, Astrid pushed down the panic and forced herself not to immediately scramble away from Logan. If she moved without waking him, she'd avoid mortifying herself, because she had the vague recollection of being the one to invite him to lie beside her. Had she really been so bold? What had she been thinking?

Besides, if she didn't wake him, then she could tend to any of the remaining patients and alleviate his burden and allow him to sleep longer. She wouldn't be back to her normal strength and stamina, but she was ready to resume her life.

Even as she gently began to inch her leg out from Logan's, he released a labored sigh and this time made circles low on her back. His fingers moved absently, the rhythm steady and gentle.

Her body gave a sudden shout of protest at leaving him. In fact, every cell in her back was inviting her to linger there with him, sending sweet tingles all over her skin that made her want to beg him to caress her everywhere.

But no. They had to move apart. It was time. In fact, it was past time.

She slipped her leg out from between his and started

to shift back, but his fingers from his other hand slid up and dug into her hair, as if he was settling in and never planning to leave.

The possessiveness of his hold wrapped deeply around her, tying her into knots and holding her captive so that she couldn't have moved even if she'd wanted to—which she didn't.

The house was still quiet. No one was yet stirring. A few more minutes next to him wouldn't hurt, would it? She'd just lie against him and relish the closeness, a proximity she hadn't ever expected with him but that she could admit was quickly becoming her favorite thing in the world.

She let herself relax again. But before she could settle in, he bent in and pressed a sleepy kiss to her cheek. A tender brush. Likely meant to reassure her that everything was alright.

Yet the softness and warmth of his lips was like an ocean current lapping against her, warm and sultry. The current tugged at her, as if to pull her out into the deep sea where anything could happen.

Leaning into the crook of his neck, she nuzzled her nose against him first, relishing the rough layer of scruff. Then before she could overthink the situation or convince herself to move away, she let her lips graze his neck. After all, if he could kiss her cheek, she could kiss his neck. Couldn't she?

She hardly brushed him, but she tasted of the roughness of his skin, the unshaven scruff, the hard lines of his jaw. Strangely, that small taste only made her hungrier for more of him. She was like a poor beggar sitting down to a banquet. She didn't want just another taste. She wanted a whole meal.

But hadn't she just warned herself that she had to get out of bed?

His breathing quickened near her ear, and his fingers slid deeper into her hair. Was he awake?

As his hand splayed out against her back, pressing her closer, she couldn't keep from taking another taste of his jaw. He was so delicious that she kept on going, making a trail across his jaw until she reached his neck. She easily found his pulse. The throbbing was hard and steady and strong. And she kissed the spot gently.

He released a soft moan.

The sound unbolted the gate holding back the rest of her reserves, and her pulse began to race like a graceful but powerful Thoroughbred, plunging forward across the open grassland. She kissed him again, this time moving lower, brandishing a trail until she reached his collarbone.

"Astrid." He whispered her name like a reverent prayer.

One of her hands skimmed up his ribcage, pressing harder with each inch, as though she could claim all of him.

He released another moan, this one ending with a hoarse whisper. "Dash it."

She needed to rein in, but this pleasure with Logan was unlike any other she'd known. And she wanted more. Endless amounts more.

As though sensing that she was on a runaway course, he pulled back and broke the connection of her kiss.

Her hand fisted into his shirt, and she shamelessly began to drag him back.

But in the next instant, he rolled away, scrambled off the opposite side of the bed, and rapidly paced to the window. He stood in front of the open pane, and the growing light of dawn outlined him, giving form to his broad back, stiff and straight, his shoulders rising and falling in quick succession and his fingers jammed into his hair.

She pushed up to her elbows, half-tempted to throw off the covers, slip out of bed, and go to him so that she could wrap her arms around him, embrace him, and feel his body against hers once more.

Oh yes, her attraction to this man was alive and well. It always had been, but the past two weeks had brought it out from the gates and paddocks that had been restraining it. But what was she doing letting it run wild and free? She had no right to do so. Especially because it would only lead to heartache for both of them.

"Astrid?" Logan's voice was low and laden with desire.

"Yes." She wasn't sure what he was asking her, but whatever it was, her answer was already yes.

"I don't want any of this between us to be fake anymore."

Had it ever been fake? Maybe she'd tried to keep it that way, but she'd obviously failed.

"My mother wants to move up the wedding date. She's actually planning on it happening at the end of this week on Saturday so long as you're strong and well enough." Finally he turned, and his dark expressive eyes beckoned to her. "I want to marry you then. Not to please her, but because I want to . . ."

Just a second ago, she'd thought she could say yes to him for anything. But she couldn't say yes to this, could she? To marrying him?

His gaze remained on her, the shadows of dawn darkening his features. Was he serious? Did he truly want to marry her?

A tiny thread of pressure tickled at the lining of her throat. The memory of the coughing spell from last night rushed back into her mind—how she'd been unable to stop, how Logan had picked her up and taken her to the window, how he'd stood with her in his arms until finally her cough had subsided.

The coughing spells were beginning to happen more frequently. Soon—if her consumption was anything like it had been in the past—it would take over her life. She'd grow too weak to look after herself.

If she agreed to marry Logan, she would just end up being a burden during her last days. He'd be stuck taking care of her, worrying about her health and always wondering how long they had.

The other truth was that she'd leave him a widower. And she couldn't do that—not to any man. Maybe that's why she'd never seriously considered marriage—not just because men were threatened by a woman doctor, but because ultimately, she would cause heartache to a husband and any children she might leave behind.

Logan took a step back toward the bed but then stopped. "Please consider it, Astrid."

"I can't—"

"I love you." His words were heavy with urgency and pleading. "I want to marry you because I love you."

The declaration should have made her giddy with happiness, should have unleashed more passion inside her. She would have given up everything long ago to hear those words from Logan. But as the pressure of the tickle in her throat swelled, so did her resolve. "It won't work between us, Logan—"

"It will, I vow it."

"No, you don't understand. With my consumption coming back, I'm only going to get sicker."

"Once we're back in Boston, I'll hire the best medical doctors in the world to look after you."

"I came here to Colorado because I need the fresh, healthy air that the higher altitude provides."

He was silent, and she could almost hear his thoughts whirring.

"I need the air here." She spoke quietly, hoping he'd understand without her having to say more.

"I have a friend with some land outside of Boston. I'll buy it from him and build you a house there where the air is fresh. It's near the ocean, and I heard the ocean is good for consumption."

She shook her head. "I'm staying here in Colorado, Logan. I'm not leaving."

"Then I'll stay—"

"No!" Her voice came out louder than she intended. She dropped to a whisper. "No, I won't let you give up your life and all of your plans for me."

"What if I want to?" He rubbed the back of his neck.

"I know you don't want to. You're ready to go back, and you're excited about the lecturing position."

"That was before I met you."

She wanted to stand up, stalk over to him, and shake sense into him. Couldn't he see that, even if he was well intentioned now, he'd eventually realize how much he'd sacrificed for her? Maybe he'd even come to resent her for having to give up his dreams.

Besides, didn't he remember how much he'd disliked living in Colorado as a youth? He'd hated it and had been in such a hurry to leave he hadn't even told her goodbye.

"I won't let you give up your plans any longer than you have. You've already sacrificed to take care of your mother and watch her die."

"Then come east with me. I promise we can make it work."

Was it possible she could find healing anywhere? Not just in the mountains? That maybe the fresh ocean air could work miracles too?

For a few heartbeats, she let her mind wander over the possibilities—the house near the ocean, the life together as man and wife. But then the reality crashed back over her—the reality of how sick she would eventually become until she was bedridden and unable to do anything for herself.

"No. I refuse to put you through more months, maybe years, of living with another invalid." She spoke louder, more firmly. "I can't marry you. I won't marry you, Logan. Please put the idea from your mind."

With that, she rolled over so that she couldn't see him.

He was quiet for long moments, his frustration filling the small room.

She hated that she was having to reject him, hated that she had to snuff out the beautiful relationship that had sprung to life again between them. But in her heart, she knew this was for the best, even if it was painful in the short term.

The silence stretched out, the pain in her chest growing with each ticking second.

"Tell me how you really feel." Finally he spoke, his whisper laced with tension. "If you can honestly say that you don't love me, then I promise I'll walk away and never bother you again."

She couldn't honestly say that. In fact, if she were truthful, she knew her feelings for Logan had never died and that they'd been all too easily resurrected with their reunion. But what was one more lie among the many she'd already told since the start of their deceptive relationship?

She pinched her eyes closed and then willed herself to say what she knew she had to in order to sever the ties with Logan and give him his freedom. "I care for you, but I don't love you."

He drew in a ragged breath, one that was laced with hurt.

Tears pricked the backs of her eyes. She loathed that she was causing him pain. But she couldn't let him sacrifice his life for her. She loved him too much to let him do that.

"You're certain?" His question prodded her to change her mind, to give them a chance.

She held herself rigid to keep from jumping out of

bed and throwing her arms around him and telling him that she'd do anything and go anywhere for him. "I'm certain, Logan. And now I think it's best if you go and we don't see each other again."

He remained motionless, almost as if her words had paralyzed him.

More tears stung and this time slipped out and ran down her cheeks. She had to assure him this parting of ways wasn't his fault, that he was a good man, that any woman would be fortunate to have him. But before she could formulate any words of assurance, his footsteps crossed toward the door. The echo was hard, almost angry. There wasn't a pause, not even a stop to say goodbye, as he strode into the hallway and then down the stairs.

As his steps echoed throughout the house, she pictured him moving through the living quarters below and then to the door. The door opened, then closed quietly.

As soon as he was outside, she sat up in bed and let the tears roll down her cheeks. Not more than five minutes later, she could hear him riding out of the barn, then past the house and down the lane.

He'd ridden out of her life again. But this time, she'd been the one to reject him and send him away.

Anguish sliced deep through the tender layers of her heart, severing it and cutting off circulation. She grasped her chest but could do nothing to alleviate the sharp wound.

She'd done the right thing. She really had. Even if it was the hardest thing she'd ever done.

19

Astrid refused to admit that she was still weak. Instead, she plunged the shovel under the muck, lifted it, and dumped it into the waiting cart.

With her arms and legs both trembling from the exertion, she paused and leaned against the railing of the horse stall. She needed to get back in bed and allow herself to recuperate properly, but after parting ways with Logan earlier, she'd been restless, so much so that when the Courtney sisters had started their morning chores, she'd gotten dressed and joined them.

Of course, they'd protested and told her she needed to be abed along with the handful of remaining patients. But the ache in Astrid's chest was too painful, and if she went back to bed, she'd only end up sobbing into her pillow.

She was better off staying busy and keeping her mind occupied to ward off thoughts of Logan.

The early morning light slanted through a high round

window to bathe the interior of the barn in soft amber. It glowed upon Patience sitting on the low stool, stooped near the udder as she milked one of the goats. The tinkling squirt of milk hitting the bottom of a tin pail brought Astrid a measure of comfort.

Patience shot a curious glance at Astrid but didn't ask any questions. Had the Courtney sisters been awake when she and Logan had their conversation? Or worse, had the passionate discussion roused the sisters, so that they'd heard everything?

Even if not, they were obviously aware that Logan was gone. Astrid hoped they believed he'd left because of his other obligations. She wasn't ready to admit to anyone that her relationship with Logan was over.

Drawing in a deep breath, Astrid hefted the shovel up only to burst into a cough. The tickle she'd experienced in her throat earlier in the bedroom hadn't gone away. In fact, now that she'd worked in the barn among the hay and dust, she'd probably only irritated her airways more.

She swallowed and tried to push the tickle down. But it rose again, this time so forcefully she couldn't stop it. Her knees buckled, and she dropped into the scant layer of hay left in the stall.

Before she could move, Patience was at her side, clutching her arm and assisting her up to her feet. "We should get you back to your bed."

She didn't want to go back to bed, but she allowed

Patience to guide her away from the stall. The cooler, humid air of the previous night had soothed her airways. Maybe it would again. "Take me—to the—creek," she managed between coughs.

As Patience walked her out of the barn into the open yard that led to the house, Felicity and Charity both stepped out of the back kitchen door, shielding their eyes with their hands to see past the low morning sun. Worry creased both of their lovely faces.

Charity tossed a hand towel back inside the kitchen, then hastened across the yard while tossing instructions to Felicity. "Warm up some of the tonic in the small pot on the stove. And then go to town for Dr. Steele."

"No," Astrid called out. "Do not—fetch—Logan."

Charity's eyes filled with concern. "He would want to know and come help—"

Astrid could only shake her head, couldn't formulate the words she wanted. She didn't want to burden Logan anymore, couldn't involve him, needed to let him go. For both of their sakes. She'd told him it would be easier if they didn't see each other and continue to stir and stoke the attraction. And even though she longed for him, she had to stick to what she'd said.

With Charity on one side and Patience on the other, Astrid stumbled along a well-worn path through the woodland to reach the creek. The rushing waterway was at least two wagon beds wide, clear and clean and cold.

For the end of July, the water was still running high. But the rocky bottom with its many pebbles was easy to see, especially in places touched by the early morning rays.

Between her bursts of deep coughing, the rustling water greeted her as she settled onto a fallen log along the edge. With each hack, her lungs burned and the fire rose into her throat, and the memories of the previous evening came back in small shards like the sunlight breaking through the aspen leaves overhead. Logan holding her against his chest. His fingers gently combing back her hair. The determination in his rigid body. The patience in his tone as he'd coached her breathing.

Oh, how she missed him, and she'd only been apart from him for a couple of hours at the most. How would she be able to go on without him forever?

As Charity and Patience knelt beside her, fresh guilt crept in. Astrid wanted to tell the two sisters to return to the house, to leave her be, to let her handle the coughing spell by herself. But she knew she couldn't. She wasn't safe alone, needed to have someone beside her.

But that wasn't fair to the sisters. Even though they'd turned their boardinghouse into a hospital and had served without complaint, they didn't need her there causing them more work because of her illness.

Even though she'd known at some point she would need to live with Greta, she didn't want to impose on anyone. Not Logan, not the Courtney sisters, not even her family. She wanted to be able to take care of herself just as she always had.

As she struggled to breathe in a full lungful, a call of her name wafted in the air from the direction of the house. Had Logan returned? Had he decided to pursue her anyway and not allow her to push him away? He was stubborn like that, but her rejection had been serious and final. And besides, once he had time to think about all her reasons for refusing him, he'd see that she was right—that his place was in the East, not here in Fairplay giving everything up for her.

Another call echoed in the shadows of the woodland, and this time, Astrid knew who it belonged to—Greta. Her sister had likely ridden out first thing this morning, anxious to check on whether she'd truly recovered from the influenza. And now she'd find out the truth that Astrid was sick with something even worse.

Astrid scrambled to stand, tried to gulp in air, tried to force the aching in her throat and chest away so Greta wouldn't discover that the consumption had returned. But as Greta ducked under a pine bough and stopped along the edge of the creek beside them, her gaze took in Astrid and the two Courtney sisters on either side of her holding her up.

Astrid waited for Greta's eyes to fill with surprise and worry and frustration. But she only paused a moment before assessing the situation and issuing more instructions for hot tea, herbal tonics, and damp towels.

Charity and Patience raced off to do Greta's bidding. And Greta gathered Astrid into her arms and settled back down on the log. Greta's soothing voice and gentle fingers upon Astrid's flushed face brought her a measure of peace, as it always had in the past. And within minutes she was resting comfortably, tucked in the crook of Greta's arm and leaning her head on her sister's shoulder, the worst of the coughing spell over.

Weak and tired, Astrid breathed in Greta's sweet, fruity scent and relished the solidness of this strong and beautiful woman who had been more like a mother to her than a sister.

"I'm sorry I didn't tell you about my consumption returning," Astrid finally whispered above the fluttering of the leaves and the unending murmuring of the river.

Greta leaned her head against Astrid's but didn't say anything.

"I was hoping once I got here it would get better and go away so that I wouldn't have to bother or worry you . . ."

"You could never bother me—"

"I've always been a bother." The words were laced with a lifetime of despair. "My own family didn't want me." After her mother had died, her older stepsiblings hadn't wanted her in the house any longer, were annoyed by the coughing and the constant care she'd needed.

She'd heard their complaints and concerns even when they'd tried to hide it from her.

"Oh, Astrid." Greta's tone was laced with regret, as if she were somehow to blame. But Greta had been the only one who'd accepted her with her sickness, who'd looked after her, had rearranged her entire life, even moving to Colorado as a mail order bride in order to provide her a new home.

"I don't want to be a burden any longer." The pain of the rejection from her family stung more than it had in a long time. A lump pushed up into her throat, and tears pricked her eyes. "And I don't want you to rearrange your life for me again. Once was enough—"

"Not for me." Greta shifted and reached for Astrid's chin. Greta's eyes were glassy, her brows drawn, and her lip trembled. "I'll never, never consider you a burden. Do you understand? Never."

A tear trickled down Astrid's cheek, but she didn't have the strength to wipe it away. "Don't say that, Greta. You know how much work my consumption will be."

Tears spilled over onto Greta's cheeks too. "You're my sister, my family. And that's what we do for one another. We sacrifice and we love and we stay by each other's sides through everything that life throws our way."

"You're already busy enough."

"Is that why you're staying here at the boardinghouse? Instead of coming home?"

More tears trailed Astrid's cheeks. "I thought I had more time."

"You're coming home with me today, do you understand?"

Astrid nodded. It was for the best. At least for the time being.

Greta brushed at the tears on Astrid's cheeks. "Does Logan know?"

The ache in Astrid's heart swelled. "Yes, he knows. But I have to tell you something. The truth about Logan and me."

Greta waited, her silver-blue eyes clear and kind and full of patience.

"Our relationship is a business arrangement. He needed someone to court in order to prevent his mother from sending away for a bride for him. And I needed the job as his partner. We agreed to help one another out."

Greta brushed her thumb across another tear. "And . . .?"

"And the whole situation quickly got out of hand when his mother assumed we were engaged. Logan didn't want to correct her, wanted her to be happy during her last days, so we went along with everything she planned and have been lying to everyone this whole time."

Greta's eyes started to crinkle, and she bit her lip, as if trying to conceal a smile.

"It's not funny, Greta."

Greta nodded, tried to work her expression into a serious one, but then a laugh bubbled out. She quickly captured it behind her hand, but her eyes sparkled with mirth, even as the tears from moments ago clung to her eyelashes.

Maybe the way Astrid's relationship with Logan had transpired was a little funny. Astrid allowed herself to smile, but then a sob rose swiftly and escaped.

Greta's smile faded and her brows furrowed. "What happened?"

Astrid swallowed the pressure of more sobs, even as the heartache of losing Logan tore at her. "This morning he told me he loved me and wanted to marry me for real."

"It's obvious how attracted you are to each other."

She was attracted to him, always had been, and was even more so now. "It doesn't matter. I'm not marrying him."

Greta grew silent.

When Astrid glanced up at her sister to read her reaction, Greta's eyes held only compassion.

Astrid's eyes stung again. "I can't go back east with him. And I won't let him sacrifice everything he's worked so hard to attain in Boston in order to stay here with me."

"Or maybe you're just rejecting him first because you're afraid he'll eventually reject you the way others have because of your consumption."

Was that what she was doing? "No. He deserves better

than me. That's all."

"I think you should give him a chance, Astrid. He really does love you. He told me so himself."

Astrid laid her head back on Greta's shoulder. Had she done the right thing in sending him away? What if she'd been too hasty? What if Greta was right, that she should have given him a chance? "It's that I care about him too much to let him suffer and watch me die. He's had enough heartache with his mother."

"Or maybe God put Logan into your life because, with his experience and knowledge, he'll be able to walk the rest of this journey with you every step of the way."

"I can't ask him to do that." Astrid twisted the engagement ring with the blue gemstone. "I *won't* let him do that."

Greta was quiet for a moment, then spoke again. "You don't have to decide today. But I do want you to come home with me and let me help you from now on. Okay?"

"Okay." It was time to go home. And it was time to break all ties with Logan—even if Greta didn't think it was. On the way to Healing Springs Ranch, she'd stop by the doctor's office and return the engagement ring.

As hard as that would be, she had to do it now before she changed her mind.

Logan didn't care that Astrid had told him she didn't want to see him again. He was going out to the Courtney Boardinghouse anyway.

He finished unlocking the door to the doctor's office and nodded hello to several people passing by before stepping inside.

Stale hot air with the hint of blood and lye greeted him, the sign that the place had been locked up for too long. He'd intended to open the clinic for the afternoon, but all morning as he'd visited those recovering from the influenza, the pressure had been building inside him—the need to visit Astrid and try again to convince her to give them a chance.

He couldn't give up yet. He hadn't imagined her interest. And he hadn't imagined her hesitation when he'd asked if she loved him. Maybe she hadn't admitted it, but he wanted to believe her feelings for him were as strong as his.

He dropped his medical bag beside the door, then stalked across the empty waiting room and into his office. After the past week of rushing everywhere and trying to save as many people as possible, the place was a mess. Empty tonic bottles and crumpled medicine wrappers littered the writing desk. Unopened mail and new medical journals lay scattered over the examining table where he'd hastily tossed them. A stack of dirty towels sat beside the back door, waiting for laundering.

Amidst the chaos, a single white envelope caught his attention. It was propped against the lantern on the writing table, and it had his name written in neat penmanship across the front.

His pulse lurched to a stop. It had to be from Astrid. He wasn't familiar with her handwriting, but she was the only other person who had a key to the office.

He hadn't seen any sign of her as he'd been walking through town just a little while ago. She must have delivered it earlier, perhaps had even come by to talk to him. What if she'd changed her mind? What if she wanted to make things work between them after all?

His heart started again, this time galloping forward. In two strides he crossed to the desk, grabbed the letter, and tore open the seal. As he fumbled to remove the slip of paper, something bulky brushed against his fingers.

With the note in hand, he tipped over the envelope,

and a ring fell into his palm. Not just any ring. It was her engagement ring.

He could only stare at it, a strange emptiness seeping inside him. She hadn't visited to tell him she loved him and wanted to be with him. No, she'd left the ring to inform him that she was serious about cutting off their relationship.

And her note?

His fingers tightened around the paper. He wanted to crumple it without reading it and show her what he thought of her decision. But he needed to understand why. Needed to know how she could give up what they had.

Yes, she thought she was being noble in not wanting him to give up his ambitions in the East, not wanting him to rearrange his life for someone else as he had for his mother, not wanting him to suffer another loss.

But he loved her enough that he didn't care about any of that. The truth was, she was more important than his plans and aspirations and his comfort and well-being. They'd already wasted long years apart, and he didn't want to miss another minute of being together—needed to make the most of the time they had left.

Expelling a tight breath, he flapped open the letter. It was only two sentences long: *I officially resign as a partner in the practice of Doctor Logan Steele. Please accept my apologies for any inconvenience this may cause.*

"No." The word echoed in the silence and heat of the room. "No, I don't accept your ring or your resignation."

His fingers closed about the paper tightly, and he balled it up. With a growl, he tossed it hard against the opposite wall. It pinged against the model of the skull before bouncing onto the floor.

He wound his way out of his office back into the waiting room. He'd go out and see her right now and tell her she had to change her mind.

Midway through the room, his footsteps faltered. What if he needed to be patient? Or . . . what if he needed to go about courting her properly this time, instead of the cooked-up shenanigans he'd perpetuated?

The worst thought of all—what if she was right and they were better off not pursuing anything?

He rubbed the back of his neck to ease the tension accumulating there. But nothing eased. Instead, his muscles tightened.

Yes, he'd been too hasty in pushing Astrid to marry him for real. As much as his heart was aching with need for her, he'd only hurt her all the more if he married her and then neglected her.

With a sigh, he lowered himself into one of the chairs. The truth lay heavily upon him alongside despair. He couldn't marry Astrid. Not now. Maybe not ever.

He stared out the dusty front window at Fairplay's main thoroughfare, which wasn't overly busy at the early afternoon hour. He'd put off doing the hard thing long enough. And now he needed to go do what he should have all along.

He tilted his head back, closed his eyes, and fought off his exhaustion. Then he leaned forward, elbows on his knees and face in his hands. Neither position brought him any measure of comfort. And stalling wouldn't make the task ahead any easier.

"Dash it all," he whispered, standing up. He may as well go now and get it over with.

He retrieved his bag, exited, and locked the door behind him. Then he started down the plank walkway toward home. His footsteps slowed the closer he drew. But he forced himself to keep going, making his conversations short with those he passed, until at last, he ducked through the trellis archway and started up the front walkway.

The parlor window was open, and voices wafted outside. Though his mother hadn't improved any over the past week, thankfully she hadn't gotten worse. Earlier in the day, he'd informed her that Astrid was better. Of course, he hadn't said anything about the consumption or Astrid sending him away.

And now he suspected she was busy with more wedding planning.

As he entered the house and stepped into the parlor, he braced himself.

At the sight of him, his mother paused in the middle of rattling off a list of menu items to the cook—likely for the special wedding feast she wanted to have.

Lying upon her chaise sofa, she was attired in a day gown instead of a bathrobe, and her hair was fixed in an elegant but simple knot. Her face was without wrinkle or worry, as if his news this morning of Astrid's recovery had given her an extra boost of energy.

He loathed that he would have to disappoint her and perhaps put worry back on her face.

As if seeing the dread or perhaps the gravity of his expression, his mother sent the cook on her way. Logan closed the parlor door and then drew up a chair beside his mother.

The draperies were open, letting in bright sunlight that fell across her. Even with the warmth, a maidservant had draped a thick blanket over her lap.

"What is it, Logan?" She reached out a hand from underneath the cover toward him.

He took it and kissed it as he settled himself in his chair. "Mother, I have a confession to make."

She waved her hand at him before tucking it back under the blanket. "No confessions. I have no wish to hear anything tiresome. Only happy things. Please."

He expelled a weary sigh. "I'm afraid this isn't happy news."

She closed her eyes. "Then you must stay silent."

Had his mother always avoided difficult conversations like this? Had they ever talked about serious matters? Or had she steered their discussions away from addressing any issues of the heart?

He met her gaze, one full of strength but warning. As much as he wanted to acquiesce as he'd clearly learned to do with her, he had to speak up or make an even bigger fool of himself when Astrid didn't show up at the wedding on Saturday.

"Mother." Not only did he have to explain that the wedding wouldn't take place, but he had to admit the truth about setting up the fake relationship with Astrid.

"It's a lovely day today." Mother shifted her attention to the open window and the clear blue skies beyond. "I do so love that about Colorado, don't you, Logan? The fact that it storms mightily one moment, but that the storms never last long. The beautiful sunshine always comes back out."

"I regret to inform you I won't be marrying Astrid on Saturday."

She waved a hand at him impatiently. "Nonsense. You most certainly will."

"No, really." He pushed down the anxiety that was tapping louder in his chest. "I must confess that I completely fabricated the relationship with Astrid from the start in order to prevent you from sending away for that woman from the East."

There. He'd said the truth. What would his mother do now? He braced himself for tears, for pleading, for demands. Instead, she smiled. "Of course you did."

He opened his mouth to say more. Then he sat back in his chair, his mind whirling.

"I might be losing the strength in my body, but I'm not losing the sharpness of my mind."

"But how could you know?"

"After all these years, I can spot when you're not being honest."

He released a groan and then buried his face in his hands.

"I won't hold it against you if you don't hold my forwardness against me."

"Of course not. Wait, what forwardness?"

"I knew you weren't engaged, but I pushed for the engagement party anyway."

He studied his mother, her lips still tilted in a small smile without a trace of remorse. "If you knew our relationship was a ruse, then why have you been pushing us so hard to get married?"

"Because I also realized you needed a big nudge in that direction. And honestly, I couldn't pick a better woman than Astrid. She's perfect for you."

Yes, she was perfect in absolutely every way. "I've lost her." The words wrenched from him and contained all the despair that had taken up residence in his heart since leaving her.

"You haven't lost her. Not yet."

"She has consumption, Mother."

"I realize that."

"You do?"

"I spoke with Greta last week and learned everything about Astrid that I didn't already know."

He should have guessed his mother would investigate more about the woman he planned to marry.

"Greta mentioned that Astrid battled the consumption as a child and survived it, but that it's possible the illness could flare up again."

"It's already flaring up."

"Then all the more reason to marry her soon."

"Or maybe she's right, that we're better off going our separate ways. I don't want to end up treating her the way Father has treated you."

The smile slid from his mother's face.

Deuces. He shouldn't have said anything about his father. Some things were better left buried deep. "I'm sorry. I shouldn't have brought it up. I know it's painful for you—"

"Since we're being truthful with each other . . ." She sank back farther into her pillows, a fresh look of pain tightening her features.

"Don't say anything more now." He started to rise. "You need to rest."

"Wait." Her bony fingers snaked around his wrist and

stopped him, forcing him to sit back down. She dragged in a breath, then spoke again. "Your father has never treated me with anything other than complete love and consideration."

"He abandoned us to come here, left us without looking back."

"No, he didn't. Your father—well, he was rising in popularity among the political circles around Boston. But he ended up on the wrong side of a fight with a political adversary. And let's just say your father had no choice but to leave Boston or bring harm to his family—to your Uncle Lloyd and his other brothers. He begged me to come with him, but I refused, was too stubborn to face the unknown wilderness."

His father hadn't left of his own free will? And he'd begged Mother to come? "He told everyone he was going to the West to search for gold."

"It was the excuse he needed to keep from ruining his family's good name."

Why hadn't Uncle Lloyd ever said anything in all the years they'd worked together? Unless he hadn't known about the threats.

Logan's mind spun with all the memories of his father's last days in Boston. How had he missed so much of what had been happening between his parents? He'd only been six years old at the time, but why hadn't his father told him more? Why hadn't his father ever tried to defend himself?

Logan could guess without having to ask. His father hadn't wanted to make his mother look bad, had protected and honored her even when it had made him appear weak.

"He wrote to me faithfully every week and told me all that he was doing to make a new home for us. But I wouldn't consider the move."

"But you said he abandoned us."

"I was angry and bitter, especially toward your father. When I suggested divorce, he told me he'd move back to Boston to be with us regardless of the consequences."

Logan dropped his head into his hands, wanting to block out everything his mother was revealing. He'd thought they'd been a team against Father, thought she'd felt the same pain of rejection he had. But in reality, she'd been the one to reject her husband. In doing so, she'd planted the discord that had festered in their family for so many years.

"I finally agreed to come for your sake." Her voice was weary, the conversation clearly taxing her.

Regardless, he couldn't stop himself from pressing her for more information. He needed to know everything. "But after we moved here, Father was always too busy for us."

"He was a busy man, has always wanted to make a difference in the lives of people. Even then, he tried to make us a family again, tried to make me happy. But I couldn't ever forgive him for leaving me."

Logan hadn't ever been able to forgive his father for leaving either. He'd carried his own anger and bitterness all these years. Maybe that was a sign he was in more danger of becoming like his mother than his father.

Still, Father was away now when Mother most needed him. "With your cancer diagnosis, instead of being with you, he's off playing politics in Denver."

She lowered her head, but not before he glimpsed the guilt in her face. "He accepted the senator position last summer because he wanted to move me to Denver to be closer to the hospital and doctors and specialized care."

"Why didn't you go with him?"

She twisted her hands together before meeting his gaze. "I wanted to spend my last days with you. And I knew if I stayed here in Fairplay, you'd come back to take care of me."

What in the deuce? She was more manipulative than he'd ever realized.

He stood abruptly as a rush of emotions roiled inside him, like the beginning of an avalanche threatening to crash down and wreak havoc.

"Say something, Logan." His mother's plea was plaintive.

But he couldn't fathom all her deception over the years, the way she'd used him, the anger she'd fostered inside him toward his father. And although his father had tried to reach out, Logan had always scoffed at the efforts, telling himself that his father deserved to feel some of the same hurt that he'd inflicted on them.

Except that his father hadn't intended to inflict hurt. He had made an effort. Greta had been right when she'd talked about how Mayor Steele had missed his family and had wanted them to move to Colorado.

Logan stuck his hands into his pockets, unable to meet his mother's gaze. "I need to go." Then without another word, he stalked across the parlor, crossed the hallway, and pushed his way outside.

He needed time and space to process all the revelations, in a place away from his mother's control.

Maybe it was time for a trip to Denver. He'd replenish his dwindling medicinal supplies, visit with a colleague who had recently become head of City Hospital, and gather all the latest news in the medical profession.

And while he was there, he'd pay his father a visit.

21

"You miss him terribly, don't you?" Catherine asked from the hot spring beside her, completely submerged like Astrid so that only her head was above the water.

Astrid peered up at the evening sky, which was glowing a soft blue and turning almost lavender with the coming of darkness. But all she could see was Logan, arms crossed and leaning against a doorframe, his dark eyes burning into her with desire.

Yes, she missed him so much her body ached because of it. But she couldn't admit her desperation to Catherine.

Astrid rested against the smooth stones, the water bubbling around her. Even though she'd relished the past few days of soaking in the natural spring several times a day, the week had crawled forward slower than a tortoise traveling uphill.

Dylan and Catherine had come out to the ranch for

supper a short while ago, and now Dylan was keeping watch over their passel of children while Catherine joined Astrid in the hot spring. Astrid was relieved to have the company, suspected Greta had invited the couple to visit for that very reason.

Catherine's sharp eyes wouldn't release Astrid's, and instead she waited for Astrid to unburden herself and share how she was doing now that she was living with Greta at Healing Springs Ranch, away from Logan.

"Since you are forcing me to admit to it, I will." Astrid breathed in a deep lungful of the steam rising from the pool. The scent of sulfur clung strongly to the air as always, as did the smokiness of the fire pit at the bathhouse where other guests were warming and drying themselves before changing back into their garments.

"Are you admitting to missing him or loving him or both?" Catherine persisted, her brown hair swept up but strands sticking to her flushed face.

They were both wearing the bathing costumes Greta had taken great pains to provide for her guests. The short skirt fell to the knees above pantaloons. And the sleeves of the bodice didn't even touch the elbows. The attire was scandalous.

Astrid swished her legs around in the deliciously warm water. "I confess I expected him to make an effort to visit me by now."

"I thought he would at least say goodbye."

"Goodbye?" Astrid sat up so quickly the evening air sent goosebumps prickling over her skin. "What do you mean? Is he leaving?"

"The doctor's office has been closed for the past three days, and the word around town is that he left late Monday afternoon."

Astrid's chest constricted, and a tickle worked up into her throat. She drew in a deep breath to keep from having a coughing spell. Since arriving at her sister's home, she'd had only one episode. She guessed that was because Greta had gone into full nursing mode, making her rest, mostly outside in the shade, plying her with fresh fruits and vegetables, and preventing her from doing any work.

The rest and nourishment were helping. But the lack of activity was difficult, gave her too much time to think—especially about Logan.

A part of her was desperate enough to do anything to overcome her consumption. She would endure the boredom and restlessness if it meant she was improving. And if her condition stabilized, what would she do? Would she seek Logan out and tell him she'd move to Boston, let him build her that house near the ocean, and live every second of every day loving him?

Yet, maybe now that he'd had time to think about her sickness and his future, he'd realized he was better off without her holding him back. Because even if her consumption went away temporarily, there was always the possibility of it coming back. They'd have to live with that. And maybe that was too much for him.

"I doubt he left permanently." Catherine pushed up too, the hot water dribbling down her arms and chest. "Not when his mother is so sick."

"How is Mrs. Steele?" Astrid regretted not seeing the dear woman one last time before riding out to Healing Springs. But she'd been wary of visiting, fearing she would reveal all that had transpired with Logan, and had decided the story was Logan's to tell.

Perhaps running away again had been his way of dealing with the lies they'd perpetuated. At least now her family knew the truth—not just Greta but everyone. As hard as it had been to admit her deception, she'd explained everything the first night she'd come home.

"As far as I know, Mrs. Steele is still about the same." Catherine slapped at a mosquito. "I can't blame Logan for doing what he did to make his mother happy. I understand what it's like to live a lie in order to protect the people you love."

Catherine's introduction to her life in Colorado had started off with an enormous identity mistake that had almost destroyed her and Dylan's relationship. But they'd persevered and had now been married for six happy years.

"I'm not saying my deception was right," Catherine added hastily. "But love can sometimes break down our reserves and cause us to do things we might not otherwise consider."

"Yes, he did everything because he loves his mother."

"And he loves you too. That was incredibly clear."

"Incredibly?"

"Oh yes. Everyone saw it."

Astrid's heart warmed at the words. She slipped her shoulders back under the surface, letting the healing waters surround her.

Catherine was silent for a moment, the sure sign she was thinking and getting ready to say something serious.

Astrid appreciated her friend's wisdom. But in this case, she didn't want anyone else telling her she needed to give Logan a chance. Greta had already done that.

"Very well. I'll admit I want to be together with Logan. But I can't put him through all of this." Astrid lifted a hand out of the water and waved it over her submerged body. "My future—my life—everything is so uncertain. I can't let him live with that."

"Don't you think you should give him a choice?"

Astrid shook her head. "He's a compassionate man, and he'll let his emotions influence his decision too much."

"Of course, I don't advocate letting our emotions dictate our decisions. But over the months I've known Logan Steele, he doesn't strike me as the sort of man who falls in and out of love at whim."

Catherine was right. Logan hadn't given in to the need for a relationship previously. If he'd developed feelings for her and wanted to be with her now, then that was serious for him. How could she dismiss his feelings without taking more time to consider everything?

"If the roles were reversed," Catherine continued, "would you let an illness of his prevent you from spending what time you have left with him?"

Astrid wanted to blurt out that their roles weren't reversed, so the matter was irrelevant. But she held the comment back and instead tried to put herself into Logan's shoes. Deep inside, she knew she'd never abandon him if he became sick, that she'd need to be with him during his dying days to take care of him and spend every moment reassuring him of her love.

Was that how he felt about her?

She expelled a long sigh.

Catherine nodded. "I thought so."

"The matter isn't that simple. There are so many complications about where we would live and how to navigate the challenges we'll face."

"It is complicated. But if you love him enough, the least you can do is lay out all the issues then let him make the choice."

Astrid shuddered in spite of the heat surrounding her. The thought of giving Logan the choice was frightening. What if he decided he didn't want the hassle after all? Maybe he'd reject her . . .

And ultimately, that's what it came down to. Her fear of rejection.

Greta had been right. Astrid had been hurt by her family's rejection, and she'd been keeping people at arm's length ever since, too afraid to let anyone truly get close. Greta and Catherine were really the only ones who'd been able to push past her defenses.

Was it finally time to take the defenses down? And if she did, could she let Logan in?

Logan stood outside the elegant home his father had purchased in Denver. He'd stayed there during the weeks before and after his mother's surgery, but in the fading evening light, he saw the place in a new way.

The elegance, even the opulence, of the massive multi-storied residence was for his mother. His father hadn't bought it for himself but had picked this home for her, because he'd hoped she would love it and be happy living in Denver. He'd even had it furnished in the style his mother would appreciate, every piece of furniture, every wall hanging, every fine rug—it was all for her.

Logan lifted a fist to knock on the door but then stuffed his hand deep into his pocket. He'd had three days to think on his mother's revelations as he'd gone about his business in Denver. And with each passing day, the need to meet with his father had grown. But now that he was here, he wasn't sure what he would say or where to start.

At some point during the ride down from Fairplay, his anger toward his parents had turned into sadness—sadness for all they'd lost as a result of years of misunderstandings. And although he wanted to shift the blame to his mother now that he knew of her stubbornness, he suspected both had played a role in the demise of the marriage.

Behind him, a carriage rattled on the wide dirt street, but otherwise the well-to-do neighborhood was quiet, most of the residents already home and ensconced inside, the windows of the other enormous houses lit from within, warm and welcoming.

If only he felt warmed and welcomed. Instead, he felt like a stranger, as if most of his life he hadn't really known his father, had only known what his mother had wanted him to believe.

He glanced back to his horse, tied loosely to a lamp post. Maybe he should just go. Blowing out an exasperated breath, he pivoted and started back down the steps.

The door opened behind him. "Logan?" His father's voice chased after him. "Wait."

Logan paused.

"I didn't know you were in town." His father's statement didn't hold accusation the way it would have if his mother had spoken it. Instead, it held longing.

Had the longing been there before? And if so, how

had he missed it? Was it possible to twist a situation and see what one wanted rather than see the truth?

Logan turned to find his father had stepped onto the stoop. He was still attired in his day clothing, but his tie was hanging loose, his vest unbuttoned, and his cuffs rolled up. His dark hair, threaded with silver, was combed back as neatly as always. And his dark eyes were as serious—maybe even sad—as always.

"Come in." His father waved a hand toward the front entryway, brightly lit, revealing the beautifully decorated home that his mother had refused to live in.

Logan's heart pinched again. He took a deep breath. "I'm sorry." He may as well get right to the point of his visit.

His father's brows rose, and confusion filled his eyes.

"I've been angry with you my whole life. For many things . . ." Logan wouldn't speak ill of his mother and didn't want to blame her for everything, especially not now that she was dying. Instead, he had to take responsibility for his anger and bitterness. He should have treated his father better and with greater consideration no matter what. After all, no one was perfect.

"I understand." His father's shoulders slumped, clearly heavy underneath the burden of his guilt.

"I was naïve and ignorant of many of the issues you and Mother faced." Logan pushed forward with what he had to say. "But that's not an excuse for how I treated you. I was wrong, and I've come to ask for your forgiveness."

His father's eyes turned glassy with unshed tears. He lowered his head and didn't respond for a moment.

Logan's eyes stung with emotion.

His father cleared his throat. "Of course—" His voice broke, and he cleared his throat again. "But I hope you can forgive me too."

Logan swallowed hard past a lump. "You tried to be a good husband and father. There's nothing to forgive for that."

His father didn't look up, was silent again. He brushed at the corner of an eye and then spoke again, his voice low. "I made plenty of mistakes."

"We all have."

His father met Logan's gaze. "I'd be a very happy man to know we can move forward and be friends."

Logan blinked back the moisture in his eyes. "I would like that."

His father nodded. "I would too."

Logan shifted his sights to the foothills on the Front Range, needing to find strength to compose himself.

"You're a good man, Logan." His father's voice held a note of pride. "And you're going to make a fine husband."

Logan scuffed the tip of his shoe against the step. "About that. The wedding is called off. Astrid and I never—"

"Don't let your fears hold you back from marrying Astrid."

"Astrid doesn't want me. She sent me away." At least, that's what he'd been telling himself since riding to Denver. But maybe his father was right. Maybe he was letting fear hold him back instead. Maybe he'd always been afraid of failing and still was.

"If I could go back and do things over," his father said, "I wouldn't have let fear drive so much of what I did."

Did his father think that if he'd stayed in Boston and faced his problems, things might have been different? Maybe they would have. But there was no guarantee. In reality, there were no guarantees anything would work out perfectly. Yet that couldn't keep them—him—from trying, could it?

"She's sick with consumption," Logan confessed, "and she thinks she's doing what's best for me by pushing me out of her life." The tangled knots inside him cinched tighter as they did whenever he thought of that last morning he'd held her in the bed, the aching desire he'd experienced from her kisses upon his neck and the power of his love for her.

"But you want to be with her regardless?" His father's voice contained only understanding.

"It's really the only thing I want." The truth had hit him hard as he'd spent the past few days researching consumption, telegramming colleagues for information, and investigating all the options that were available. "No matter how much time she has left, whether it's weeks or years, I want to spend every single day by her side. The problem is, I don't know how to make it happen or how to convince her."

His father waved at the interior of the house. "Come in. I might not have all the answers. But I'd like the chance to help, if you'll let me."

Logan wasn't sure if his father—or anyone—could help. But he was desperate to figure out a way to convince the woman he loved to give their relationship another chance.

22

Tomorrow would have been her wedding day if she'd gone through with marrying Logan. Tomorrow.

With a sigh, Astrid flicked her wrist back and forth and tugged downward on the slack line, keeping it from hitting the water and scaring the fish. Ahead at the rapids, the last rays of the sun glistened on the spraying droplets, turning them into diamonds. The light also brushed the blue spruce trees that lined the bank, gilding them with silver.

Ty stood well behind her, upstream in the wide river. At fourteen, he was her oldest nephew and the best fly-fisher in the family. Astrid had asked him to bring her to their favorite spot, and Greta had reluctantly agreed to the activity as long as they didn't stay too long . . . and because she'd hoped it would take Astrid's mind off Logan's absence.

It hadn't worked. In fact, with every passing day, she

was only thinking of him more.

From what she'd heard, Logan was still absent, hadn't been seen in Fairplay all week. And rumors were starting to circulate that he wasn't coming back.

Every time she considered the possibility that he'd gone east without telling her goodbye, her chest squeezed tight, and she almost forgot how to breathe. What if he'd walked out of her life this time the same way he had all those years ago? Would she simply let him go? Or would she chase him down this time?

With expert fingers, she pulled in the line, checked to make sure the fly was on the hook, then she tossed the line behind her the way she'd learned years ago from Greta's husband. Quickly, she snapped the line forward, extending it down toward the water in a graceful arc so that the fly hovered near the surface.

The beauty of the motion, especially by the light of the setting sun, soothed the ache in her soul . . . but it didn't make it go away. She wasn't sure if her ache for Logan would ever go away, not this time.

Behind her in the cascading creek, the slap of fins against the surface told her Ty had caught another fish.

She shot a look over her shoulder.

He was standing, feet braced, fingers working furiously as he lessened the slack of his line and drew the fish upward. "Brown trout," he called, the fish's scales glinting like a rainbow.

"A beauty." She could watch her nephew fish all day. Tall and broad, his lanky body still had some filling out to do. But he was turning into a handsome man, and all the young women throughout the high country were in love with him—if Greta's motherly exaggeration could be trusted.

Astrid repositioned herself on the slick rocks beneath her. The rushing river reached almost to her knees, skimming near the top of her rubber boots, her skirt pulled up and tucked into her waist. Long gone were the days when she'd waded in bare feet and stripped down to her underdrawers to fish.

She couldn't believe she'd ever been so daring. She'd been fearless and carefree for much of her childhood, probably because of the uncertainty surrounding the recurrence of her illness and the inability to predict her long-term prognosis.

Somewhere during her growing up years, she'd become more calculated and careful. Perhaps subconsciously she'd started to believe that if she could control every aspect of her life, she'd survive longer.

Was it possible both views were flawed? That neither wild abandonment nor careful regulation would bring about the life she wanted?

She'd learned a hard truth over the years of working as a physician. Whether sick with consumption or not, a person's life could be snuffed out in the blink of an eye, and no one truly had control over when that blink happened.

Maybe instead of living in fear of the end, the key was in cherishing each day as a gift and pursuing it to the fullest with those she loved by her side.

Could that possibly include Logan?

"Dr. Nilsson." The call came from a rise on the far riverbank.

The voice belonged to none other than Logan Steele, and just the sound of it sent her pulse rushing as swiftly as the river.

She stopped flicking her wrist and let the water carry her line, and shifted so rapidly she almost slipped.

He sat atop his dark bay stallion among the spruce trees. Attired in his usual impeccable suit, he made a dashing picture, especially with the evening sun highlighting him and turning him into a bronze work of art.

He made no move to get down, and the brim of his bowler was pulled too low for her to get a glimpse into his eyes. But even with the distance, she couldn't miss the hard set of his shoulders and the rigidness of his jaw.

He slipped a hand inside his coat and pulled out a folded sheet. He held it out. "Do you know what I think of your resignation letter?"

She bumped up Ty's straw hat that she was wearing and squinted against the glint of sunlight on the water.

"This is what I think." His voice rang out above the river, and in the next instant, he was ripping the letter, first in half, then into smaller pieces, until at last he let the shreds fall from his hand into the river. The water quickly drenched the paper, and soon each slip disappeared under the surface.

"If my actions aren't clear," he said, "then let me state myself plainly. I don't accept your resignation."

A bubble of relief welled within her. He wanted her back. Even if only to help as his partner in the clinic. No, he wasn't professing his love, and no, he wasn't asking her to marry him again. But this was a start.

"Very well," she called. "Since you clearly need my assistance, I really have no choice in the matter."

From behind her, Ty muttered, "Ma ain't gonna like this. You know she wants you resting."

She shot her nephew a warning look. She'd work out the details with Greta later.

Logan was digging in his pocket. "The other thing I refuse to accept is this." He pulled out a tiny object.

She didn't have to be up close to know what it was. Her engagement ring. Her heart gave a hard kick.

He held it out, dangling it from a thin gold chain, giving her a clear view of the blue gemstone. "You might not be ready to receive this for real yet. But I intend to prove to you every day for the rest of my life why you should wear it and never take it off."

Her breath caught in her throat. Not only did he want her to work with him, but he still wanted to marry her. At the sight of him so strong and steady upon his steed, she knew there was no other man she'd ever want to marry. Logan Steele had always been and still was the man for her.

Yes. Yes. Yes. The word echoed inside, but her throat was too tight to say it.

"And yes, I have thought this through," he said. "I've already telegrammed my uncle in Boston and told him I won't be coming back. I intend to practice in Fairplay, but I also began discussing with my father plans for starting a medical college here in Colorado. He believes that's something the state legislature will support."

"A medical college?"

"And my colleague at Hospital General in Denver would like me to join him in his research on consumption. He's doing fantastic work on the disease and has plans to eventually open a sanatorium."

"That's—I don't know what to say—"

"Don't say anything right now. Please, just think about it." He nudged his horse toward the closest spruce and gently draped the chain over a branch so that it hung there like a Christmas tree ornament. "I won't stop trying to win you, but I also won't pressure you into marrying me. I did that once, and it didn't work."

She wanted to slog to the bank and let him put the

ring on right then and there. But she could only stand in the middle of the river, her fishing line now tangling in the rapids.

He dug his heels into his mount, urging the magnificent creature away from the riverbank. "When I've finally won you over, put it on. Then I'll know you're ready to marry me."

Had he already won her? She took a step toward the shore, but the flow of the river dragged against her feet. Before she could lift another foot, Logan veered his horse away from the river.

Speechless, she watched him ride, his strength evident in every fluid move.

Even after he disappeared from sight, she could only stare at the tree, both fear and desire warring within her. She couldn't deny how much she loved Logan. But could she accept his engagement ring, this time for real?

Deep inside she knew she wanted nothing more than to spend all the time she had left with him. But was that fair to him? Maybe it wasn't fair *not* to give him that choice. Catherine had encouraged her last night at the hot spring to be honest with Logan about all the implications of marrying a woman like her. If she laid it all out and he still wanted to be with her, how could she deny him?

With her heartbeat starting up again and moving sluggishly, she waded toward the shore, dragging her pole and line. She could feel Ty watching her, waiting to see what she intended to do with the ring hanging from the branch of the spruce tree.

Each step she took, her heart spurted harder and faster with both love and passion. By the time she stepped out onto the rocky bank and began to climb toward the ridge, her chest ached with the pressure growing inside.

She grabbed onto long strands of brown grass and scraggly roots until she was at the top beside the tree. Thankfully he'd hung it from a lower branch. Standing on the tips of her toes, she touched the chain and slipped it off the limb.

As her fingers closed about the chain, she let it dangle from her fingers, the low sunlight turning the gemstone on the ring pale blue, the same color as her eyes. The ring was as stunning now as it had been the night he'd kneeled before her and caressed her fingers as he placed it on.

The engagement had felt authentic that night even though it had been a show for his mother. But tonight, he'd offered her marriage again, not to please his mother, not as a part of any bargain, but because he wanted her. He wanted her enough that he was rearranging his life and plans.

The question was—was she ready?

She closed her fingers around the ring, clutching it tightly.

No one was making her do this. No one was expecting it. In fact, everyone would understand if she didn't want to have a relationship right now so that she could focus on her health.

Maybe she'd never feel fully ready. Maybe she'd always have underlying worries. But she had to take this risk, didn't she? She'd just admonished herself to stop worrying about how much time she had left and to instead cherish each day and pursue her life with those she loved by her side.

She unfurled her palm and unhooked the clasp of the chain. Then, before any other excuses could stop her, she slipped the ring down her finger. As she settled it in place, her hand trembled. Even so, she stretched it out and admired the ring back on her hand as if that's where it had always belonged.

"Reckon this means you're gonna marry Dr. Steele?" Ty's call came from the middle of the river where he still stood, his fishing line flat, his attention squarely upon her.

She loved Logan and had to give him a chance. Maybe once he heard all her concerns again, he'd change his mind. But she couldn't let fear of rejection stop her from trusting others or from opening up her life and allowing them in.

"Yes, that's what it means. We'd better get on back to Greta and let her know I'm engaged to Dr. Steele. Again."

Ty heaved an exasperated sigh as though he couldn't quite understand why she'd want to stop their fishing over an engagement. But as she pressed the ring against her heart, she knew she was doing the right thing.

Within the hour, they were back at Greta's big house, darkness settling in so that the bright lights in the windows welcomed them back. As Ty helped her down from her mount, Greta rose from the rocker on the wraparound porch, holding her youngest, now asleep. "Logan came by looking for you."

"He found us alright," Ty answered before Astrid could. "And he gave Aunt Astrid back her engagement ring."

Astrid held out her hand toward Greta, revealing the ring. "He told me he'd wait until I was ready. And I decided that whether I'm ready or not, I don't want to miss any more time with him. I want to make the most of what I have left."

"Good." Greta smiled even as her eyes filled swiftly with tears. "I want you to experience love and marriage and maybe even babies for as long as you can."

The desire for all of that rose so swiftly that tears sprang to Astrid's eyes too. Was it possible she might get to have the love and family of her own she'd always dreamed about? She didn't want to allow her hopes to rise too high, because she had to make sure Logan truly understood what marrying her would entail. Even so, excitement began to thrum through her.

Greta brushed at the silky soft hair of her youngest

before pressing a kiss against his cheek. "I'm sure Mrs. Steele would love to hear the news before she passes."

Something in Greta's tone brought Astrid's swirling thoughts to a halt. "Before she passes?"

"Didn't Logan mention it?" Greta's eyes brimmed with a sadness that told Astrid everything she needed to know.

"How long does he think she has?"

"Less than twenty-four hours."

A shaft of sorrow sliced into Astrid's heart. For Logan. Even though the end wasn't unexpected, it would still be painful for him. He needed her now more than ever, and she wanted to go to him, comfort him, and be by his side.

Greta was watching her face, as if reading each thought. "I have an idea. A way to keep you from overexerting yourself but also allow you to be with Logan during his mother's end."

"What is it?"

"It's a wild idea. But please don't say no until you hear me out." Greta leaned in and whispered a plan into Astrid's ear.

Astrid pulled back and smiled. "It's perfect. Let's do it."

23

Logan awoke with a start to bright light streaming in his bedroom. How long had he slept?

He grasped at his pocket watch on the nightstand, nearly knocked it off, then flipped open the case and squinted at the Roman numerals. It was half past eight.

With a spurt of anxiety, he jolted up in bed, shoved off the sheet covering him, and swung his legs to the floor. "Deuces," he muttered. He'd only meant to rest for an hour or two. And he'd been abed for at least four.

A soft knock was followed by the door opening a crack and his father poking his head inside. "You're awake."

Logan stood and grabbed his trousers from the bedside chair. "How is she?"

His father stepped in and closed the door behind him. "She's doing better."

"Better?" With one leg in his trousers, Logan paused.

"She's awake and wanted to go down to the parlor."

Something in his father's tone was different. And in his expression. Was it hope?

Logan finished tugging on his trousers, not sure how to tell his father that his hope was misplaced. Just because Mother was feeling better now didn't mean she would get better. In fact, some dying patients had bursts of energy just before passing, perhaps the last push to say goodbye.

"She's waiting for you." His father crossed to the large wardrobe, swung open the door, and rummaged inside before pulling out a clean shirt.

Logan had already picked up the shirt he'd worn yesterday on the ride up to Fairplay and then all of last night as he'd sat by his mother's bed. But as his father thrust the clean shirt at him, he tossed the dirty garment aside.

His father turned back to the wardrobe and opened one of the drawers inside. "She's asked the cook to prepare a brunch."

"Brunch? She won't be able to eat much, if anything." Even though Logan had been angry with his mother when he'd left earlier in the week, he'd had every day since then to let go of the resentment. When he and his father had arrived home late yesterday afternoon, he'd quickly realized just how much she'd deteriorated over the five days he'd been gone.

She'd been in bed, immobile, and mostly

unresponsive. In fact, he hadn't been sure she'd even make it through the night. He'd beaten himself up for being gone from her for so long, for leaving at all. And he'd done everything he could to revive her and make her comfortable.

The only time he'd left her side was when his father had encouraged him to ride out to see Astrid. Apparently his father had sensed his desperation to find out how she was faring and had assured him Mother would be fine for a couple of hours while he was gone.

Upon arriving at Healing Springs Ranch, Greta had come out to greet him. She'd answered his frank questions about Astrid's condition so that he'd learned with great relief that the fresh air, hot spring, rest, and healthy food were helping, and Astrid hadn't had any more coughing over recent nights.

The news had confirmed what he'd learned during his few days of researching consumption while in Denver, especially after consulting with his friend Dr. Marcus Holiday. Marcus had given him information regarding several studies, one by a scientist in Germany, Hermann Brehmer, who purported that getting patients into the pure mountain air at reduced atmospheric pressure eased the pumping action of the heart muscle and improved blood flow. Brehmer believed that those suffering from consumption should strengthen themselves physically to ward off the disease. He advocated for walks, plenty of rest, and a nutritious diet.

Marcus had also told Logan about Dr. Trudeau in New York, who'd contracted consumption several years ago. While suffering during the advanced stages of the illness, the ailing physician had decided to live his last days in the wilderness of the Adirondack Mountains. While spending his days and nights at mountain lakes, strolling in the forests, and resting extensively, his fever and night sweats had disappeared, he'd gained weight, and his cough had gone away.

Of course, Logan wasn't naïve enough to believe that such treatment would work for everyone. But he wanted to believe that it would benefit Astrid, especially since it had already helped her once as a girl.

Between Father and Marcus, he'd been able to devise plans for his own career to show Astrid that he could live anywhere and do anything and still be happy. And he'd also been able to come up with a strategy for how to treat Astrid's consumption that combined both Brehmer's and Trudeau's studies.

Whatever the case, he'd been relieved to discover from Greta that Astrid was already doing better. When he'd tracked Astrid down at the fishing spot and watched her from the banks of the river, his heart had ached with such need and love that he'd known he had to tell her again that he wanted to marry her.

He knew it would take time to convince her that he

was serious, that he wasn't abandoning her now that her consumption had returned, and that he intended to stay with her for as many days as God gave them. But he was determined to woo her and wait until she finally realized he wasn't going away this time. He was committed to her. Forever.

"Your mother is happy this morning," his father said, pulling a bow tie from the drawer.

Logan paused in buttoning his shirt. Again his father's tone held anticipation that set Logan on edge. "Listen, you have to understand that this mood of hers today can be typical of someone nearing the end."

His father tossed him the tie. "I know. But it won't hurt for us to indulge her this morning and dress our best, will it?"

For the first time, Logan took in his father's attire—a fine suit, a smart bow tie, his hair slicked back with pomade. He looked as distinguished as he had the night of the fake engagement party.

Father had no reason to indulge Mother, not after the years of her manipulation and bitterness. But he was doing it anyway for the woman he'd never stopped loving in spite of all the difficulties they'd faced. It would have been easier for his father to walk away, or at the very least to become bitter himself. Instead, he'd made the conscious decision to stay committed to his wife, even when she'd rejected him time after time.

"What is it?" his father asked as he swiped up a pair of cuff links from the drawer.

"You're a good husband. I hope someday I get the chance to commit to Astrid the way you have with Mother."

His father's lips quirked into the beginning of a smile. "I have no doubt you will."

"I hope you're right."

He hastened to finish his grooming, and within minutes, he was striding beside his father down the hallway, past his mother's now-empty room, and toward the stairway. As he reached the top, voices carried up from the parlor. One sounded distinctly like Father Zieber, the reverend of their small church.

He halted. "Did Mother invite guests to the brunch?"

"Yes. I believe so." His father was already striding down the steps. "Now, let's hurry. We can't keep her waiting any longer."

Logan's shoes tapped a quick rhythm on the tile. He wasn't sure how he felt about having guests today, quite possibly his mother's last day on earth. Perhaps she'd invited the reverend to pray with her as she prepared for death.

Logan wanted her to spend the final hours of her life peacefully. But if company was what she wanted, who was he to prevent her from having that?

He followed behind his father through the front

entryway. As he stepped into the parlor, he pulled up short at the sight of his mother lying upon the chaise sofa in her best gown, her hair elegantly coifed. Her eyes were bright, her cheeks flushed, and her smile brilliant.

"Logan." She held out a hand, the bracelets and rings clinking together, too big on her frail body.

The others in the room had ceased their conversations. He didn't bother looking at them, didn't want to waste time visiting with anyone when his time with his mother was so short.

"You look lovely today, Mother." As he reached her, he took her outstretched hand and kissed it.

"Thank you, my dear." She held out her other hand toward one of the guests, someone waiting in the shadows of the corner.

As the woman stepped forward into the morning sunshine, Logan's heart ceased beating at the sight of the porcelain face with those magical blue eyes. "Astrid?" The one word escaped, but after that he was speechless with wonder as she glided toward his mother and took her other hand.

She was attired in a stunning gown of layer upon layer of white tulle and taffeta. Her hair was coiled in long curls intertwined with tiny white flowers and seed pearls. And she was radiant, more beautiful than he'd ever seen her before.

His father, standing beside him, squeezed his

shoulder. "Breathe, Logan."

The other guests laughed lightly—guests that not only included the tall and burly Father Zieber in his clerical collar but also Greta and Wyatt along with Catherine and Dylan. None of their children were present. Not that Logan disliked the children, but for today, the smaller group for brunch would be better for Mother.

As his mother gazed up at first Astrid and then him, her smile was bigger than he'd seen in years. "You ready?"

Before he could answer, Astrid nodded. "I'm ready." As she spoke, her gaze lifted to meet his. Her eyes, as always, had the power to decimate him, knock down every defense, and render him her prisoner.

His mother did what she'd done the day of the fake engagement party and pressed Astrid's hand into his. He didn't hesitate in taking it. As he lifted Astrid's hand to his lips, he didn't break his eye contact, her eyes holding questions he didn't understand.

He bent and kissed her knuckles. His lips brushed against bare, gloveless skin. And a ring.

With a strange jolt in his chest, he dropped his sights to find the engagement ring there on her finger. His heart began to race erratically. What did this mean? Surely she wasn't telling him what he thought she was . . .

He straightened and searched her face to find that she was nibbling her lip. "You won me over."

Another jolt went straight through him—a powerful surge of joy. "I haven't done anything yet to win you—"

"You won me over the first moment I met you." The words were soft and sincere. "And now I'm ready." She was repeating what he'd told her yesterday, making sure he understood why she was there.

He couldn't contain the smile that broke free. And as he glanced around the room to all the other smiling faces, his grin only widened. The reverend, Astrid's sister, her best friend. This was a wedding. Theirs. On the day his mother had wanted. Most likely the last day of her life.

As his mother released a blissful sigh, Logan caught his father's twinkling gaze. His father had known about it, too, and had been tasked with getting him in his best suit and downstairs to the parlor.

He brought Astrid's fingers back to his lips and kissed her knuckles again, wishing he could kiss each finger slowly and languidly, but he satisfied himself that even with so small a kiss, her eyes widened, revealing her desire.

"Father Zieber," he said without taking his gaze from Astrid's face. "Shall we begin?"

"Of course." He stepped up beside them, his prayer book already open to the order of matrimony.

"Wait." Astrid pinned Logan with serious eyes. "Before you commit to me, I need you to know the realities of what you're getting into by marrying me." The gravity that fell over her expression told him that, even with all the plans he'd laid out yesterday, she was still worried that her consumption would be a barrier between them.

She started to speak again, but he pressed a finger gently against her lips and cut her off. "All marriages have challenges that can cause problems and heartache. If not consumption, it could be something else." Just like his parents' marriage. "But I promise to commit myself to you no matter how hard it will get and to love you until my dying breath."

"You're sure?" Her big eyes filled with hope.

"I've never been more sure of anything."

Her pretty lips curled into a smile. "And I promise to do the same, to commit myself to you no matter how hard it will get and to love you until my dying breath."

Father Zieber closed the prayer book. "Well, I guess that's it. Mr. Steele asked me to keep the ceremony short, and since those are the best vows I've heard in a long time, I may as well pronounce you man and wife."

"I won't complain." Logan wanted to finish as quickly as possible—for his mother's sake and so that Astrid could rest too.

"Good." Father Zieber tucked his prayer book under his arm and made the sign of the cross. "Then I pronounce that you are husband and wife, in the name of the Father, and of the Son, and of the Holy Ghost. Those whom God has joined together, let no one put asunder."

His mother laughed lightly and then clapped, and the other guests joined her. "Don't forget the kiss," his mother called breathlessly, her eyes bright with unshed tears.

Seeing the joy and tears brought a lump to Logan's throat. And at Astrid's tender smile and the tears in her eyes, he guessed she'd orchestrated the wedding so quickly because she knew how much it would mean to him and to his mother.

"Kiss her, Logan," his mother persisted.

Instead of waiting for him to comply, Astrid rose up and pressed her lips against his softly, sweetly, and shyly. The warmth and tenderness of her touch declared her love—a love she was offering him for as long as she could.

He wrapped his arms around her and brought her close, and at the same time, he replied with a kiss of his own, one that contained all his love and the promise of giving her all that he had, body, soul, and spirit, for as long as he could.

As he pulled away, keeping the kiss short, he brushed another kiss against her forehead.

His mother clapped again, and this time he bent and kissed her cheek. "I love you, Mother."

"I love you too, my dear." She leaned her head back. "Now let's celebrate with brunch, shall we?"

The scents of bacon, sausage, biscuits, and coffee

made Logan's stomach growl. Apparently the brunch hadn't been only a ruse to get him downstairs. It was part of his mother's original wedding plans. Even so . . . "You should rest."

She clasped his hand, and her gaze pleaded with him. "Give me this last day to enjoy you and Astrid together. Please? I'll never get to do this again."

Astrid laid a hand on his mother's arm. "Of course we will, Mrs. Steele—"

"Mother," she whispered. "Call me *Mother* today, will you, Astrid?"

"I will. Mother."

Several tears slipped down his mother's cheek even as she smiled up at them both.

As the servants began to bring in trays of breakfast foods and steaming mugs of coffee, Logan pulled Astrid into his arms again. He couldn't resist, doubted he'd ever be able to resist holding her every chance he had.

She came against him willingly, eagerly, her gaze hungry upon his mouth.

He bent and swiftly captured her lips, needing another kiss, needing to feel her, needing her more than anything else. There was nothing he wanted to do more than to show her every day just how much he needed her, that he always had and always would. They would face the uncertain future together, side by side. And nothing would be able to tear them apart. Not even death.

24

As the first shovel of dirt hit the casket, Astrid leaned her head against Logan's arm.

His arm around her waist tightened as he stared at the open hole in the ground, his face stoic, his eyes solemn, his lips pressed together firmly. His hold was unyielding, as though he needed her—needed her strength, needed her comfort, needed her calmness in this moment of loss.

The August afternoon was warm, the summer sun high in the clear blue sky, drying up the grass and turning the land into a brittle dusty brown for miles all around. Only a lone gnarled and blackened tree stood nearby, once known as the hanging tree during the days when vigilante committees ensured justice was served in the high country.

Ever since the brunch, Mrs. Steele had wavered in and out of consciousness, until she'd peacefully passed away yesterday afternoon. There had been nothing more they could do for her. It had been her time to go. And in the end, they would always cherish the happy memories from their wedding day, grateful that she'd been able to be a part of that happiness.

Logan's father stood next to them, and much of the community had assembled in the small graveyard just outside of town, enclosed by a tall scrolling iron fence. Even ranchers and cowhands from around South Park had come, mostly out of respect to Landry Steele.

The man had built the community from a small mining camp to the thriving town that it had become. According to Logan, his father had done it all for his family in order to make a new home and a place where he and his mother could be happy.

Logan had shared that with her during one of the many conversations they'd had over the past couple of days since their wedding as they'd kept vigil at Mrs. Steele's bedside.

They'd also made plans for Astrid to resume her partnership at the clinic, but only part time and only seeing patients in the office. He didn't want her to travel and do the home visits for fear she would become taxed and overtired.

And she'd agreed. She didn't want to do anything to jeopardize her improvement either. She'd even gone into the doctor's office for a few hours yesterday to treat some of the most pressing cases, and she'd been surprised to find that most people had been warm and accepting of her doctoring. Apparently, her dedication during the influenza epidemic had made an impression on the townspeople, especially because she'd almost died herself from all her sacrifices.

Of course, there were still the naysayers who didn't think a woman should be a doctor. They still made sure to tell her about it every chance they got.

But thankfully, she would be able to continue to do what she loved, at least for the time being. And Logan seemed content with the new opportunities that awaited him in Denver with his research as well as his involvement in hopefully starting a new medical college. He'd shared more details with her regarding all the options, the possibility of traveling there occasionally or even living there at times, but only if she came with him.

For now, though, they planned to remain in Fairplay where Astrid could continue to heal. Mr. Steele had given Logan the deed to the house and barn, including the horses. He'd wanted to give Logan the mine too, but Logan had asked his father to wait. For the time being, he wanted to focus on getting settled into his new life with his bride.

As the last of the dirt was shoveled into place, Father Zieber, at the forefront of the grave, spoke the closing words of the funeral. "When we shall depart this life, we may rest in Him as our hope as this our sister does. Grant this, we beseech Thee, O merciful Father, through Jesus Christ, our Mediator and Redeemer. Amen."

A murmuring of amens rose from around the graveyard. After a moment of silence, people began to move through the gate and walk quietly toward town, men putting their hats back on and women dabbing at their eyes.

Several prominent businessmen offered condolences to both Logan and his father. Astrid broke away from Logan when her family approached. They hugged her and spoke briefly before heading off.

At a gentle squeeze of her arm, Astrid glanced up to find Charity Courtney waiting beside the grave, regarding her with compassion, her sisters a short distance behind her. "How is your health?" The beautiful woman's brows furrowed above her caring brown eyes.

"I haven't had any more coughing." Astrid breathed in deeply, as if to prove that the irritation in her airways was gone. Even the tightness in her chest had abated.

Charity tucked a loose strand of her red hair back into her bonnet. "Good. I'm truly happy to hear it. And I'm happy to hear of your wedding, although I wasn't surprised." At her admission, her cheeks flushed.

Obviously Charity had witnessed the attraction that had flared so easily with Logan. Maybe she'd even glimpsed them in bed together that last morning. Astrid could feel herself beginning to flush at the memory too.

She and Logan hadn't shared any intimacies yet. The timing simply hadn't been right. It had been enough to be at his side. And kiss him. They'd done lots of kissing.

"You're blessed. Dr. Steele adores you." Again, Charity's cheeks flushed, and she ducked her head.

"I hope you'll find someone who adores you too." Astrid hadn't had the time to discover how the engagement dance had gone for Charity. Of course, she'd attracted the men as easily as nectar drawing a hive of honeybees. Even now, Charity and her sisters were drawing plenty of long looks from single men.

"Maybe someday." Charity didn't afford a single fellow even a glance. "For now, I'm too busy to consider any man seriously."

At the very least, the night of the dance as well as using her boardinghouse as the hospital had helped the community trust the Courtney sisters. Astrid had heard they'd gained two boarders in just the past week.

Astrid watched the sisters walk away until a body pressed against her from behind. Logan's lean but muscular body. His arms slid around her waist, and he pulled her back so that she was ensconced in his embrace, right where she belonged, the only place she wanted to be.

She breathed out a sigh of contentment that caught in her throat as his lips pressed hard against her neck. The heat of the touch seared through her body like a hot tonic.

She folded her arms across his to trap him in place behind her. Although the graveside was neither the time nor place for kissing, she suspected Mrs. Steele was in heaven hoping they would.

His lips shifted to her ear. "Charity Courtney's right, you know."

"How so?" Astrid tilted her head, suddenly breathless with need.

He didn't kiss her again, but his lips brushed her ear lobe. "I adore you."

His low whisper only added to the warmth coursing through her blood stream. "I adore you too." She hadn't yet had the opportunity to tell him she loved him. She suspected that he knew. Even so, she was long overdue in speaking the words.

She leaned back, twisting enough so that she could catch his gaze. "Logan Steele, I not only adore you, but I love you."

His dark eyes widened at her confession. And filled with happiness, the best kind of medicine for both sickness and sorrow. "I love you too." He kissed her cheek, the kiss holding the promise of much more to come.

Then, as if hearing his mother's chiding from heaven commanding him to kiss his bride, he angled in and took her lips captive in a kiss that most certainly made his mother and all of heaven smile down upon them.

Author's Note

Thank you, Readers, for coming along with me on another journey to the Colorado high country with my Colorado Cowgirl series and *Committing to the Cowgirl.* (By the way, if you haven't read the Colorado Cowboy series, make sure you go read that series when you're done with this one!)

As with all my books, it takes a huge team of people to get a book ready for publication. I seriously wouldn't be able to write as many books as I do without the help of my awesome assistant, Rel Mollet. Thank you for the many, many, many ways you help and support my writing career. You are incredible!

A huge thank you to Roseanna White for using her creativity to design the covers. You're amazingly talented! I'm so grateful for your patience as with me as we work hard to craft each cover to match the story.

Another huge thank you to my editor Katie Donovan. Thank you for always somehow managing to squeeze my books into your schedule no matter how busy you are with life and family! I have appreciated your steady dedication to helping polish my books to perfection.

Thank you to all my beta readers who are on my First Readers team! I am supremely thankful for your keen eyes in catching all those last lingering typos. Many hugs and much thanks to Zanese, Edward, Amber, Stacey, Gina, and Megann for helping me with this first book in the series.

Finally, thank you, Readers, for all your support and encouragement! If you like my sweet western historical romances, be sure to let me know. With enough interest, I might be convinced to do another Colorado series! Contact me on my website at jodyhedlund.com. Or join my Facebook Reader Room at facebook.com/groups/jodyhedlundsreaderroom.

Jody Hedlund is the bestselling author of more than forty novels and is the winner of numerous awards. Jody lives in Michigan with her husband, busy family, and five spoiled cats. She writes sweet historical romances with plenty of sizzle.

A complete list of my novels can be found at jodyhedlund.com.

Would you like to know when my next book is available? You can sign up for my newsletter, become my friend on Goodreads, like me on Facebook, or follow me on Twitter.

Newsletter: jodyhedlund.com
Facebook: AuthorJodyHedlund
Twitter: @JodyHedlund

The more reviews a book has, the more likely other readers are to find it. If you have a minute, please leave a rating or review. I appreciate all reviews, whether positive or negative.

* 9 7 9 8 9 8 5 2 6 4 9 6 8 *